KU-347-263
WITHDRAWN
FROM STOCK

Dear Reader

When Razak Khan appeared in A FAMILY TO COME HOME TO, so good-looking and charming, he was only supposed to be a minor character. Then I started wondering about him—about his background, about his career and his private life, about the things that were important to him for his future.

Then I wondered what it would do to all his plans if he were to meet someone who challenged him and how he saw that future.

To Lily, her career had been her single-minded focus since she was a young girl, so meeting a man like Razak…a man who made her aware that she was a woman as well as a surgeon…was bound to turn everything on its head. How was she going to resist him when they were spending so many hours a day in each other's company, their eyes speaking volumes over the tops of their masks without a word being said?

The obstacles between them and the way they are overcome only go to prove something I have always believed—that anything worth having is something worth fighting for.

I hope you enjoy their story as much as I enjoyed writing it.

Happy reading

Josie

Lily pressed back against the ancient wall, hoping that she would be invisible in the deep shadows of the colonnade.

She had no idea what had woken her—possibly the sound of Razak's voice through the open door that led out to the atrium…although she hadn't realised that it was open until she saw the filmy curtain billowing gently.

'Why him?' she breathed, closing her eyes tight against the threat of tears. Why did she have to go and fall in love with someone so…unattainable?

She must have made a sound, because the next thing she knew he was there in front of her, a dark silhouette against the beaten silver of the moonlit pool behind him.

'Lily?' he murmured, framing her shoulders with the gentle warmth of his hands and angling his head to peer into her face. 'You should go inside, away from the breeze,' he said. But when she thought he would usher her into her room and return to his own, he accompanied her through the gauzy curtains and turned her to face him again.

'Don't look away,' he whispered, cupping his fingers around her face and tilting it up towards his again. And she was lost, gazing into those dark eyes that had captivated her the first time she'd seen them…

SHEIKH SURGEON, SURPRISE BRIDE

BY

JOSIE METCALFE

All the characters in this book have no existence outside the imagination of the author, and have no relation whatsoever to anyone bearing the same name or names. They are not even distantly inspired by any individual known or unknown to the author, and all the incidents are pure invention.

First published in Great Britain 2007
Harlequin Mills & Boon Limited,
Eton House, 18-24 Paradise Road, Richmond, Surrey TW9 1SR

ISBN-13: 978 0 263 19786 0
ISBN-10: 0 263 19786 7

Set in Times Roman 10½ on 12¾ pt
15-0107-51578

Printed and bound in Great Britain
by Antony Rowe Ltd, Chippenham, Wiltshire

Josie Metcalfe lives in Cornwall with her long-suffering husband. They have four children. When she was an army brat, frequently on the move, books became the only friends that came with her wherever she went. Now that she writes them herself she is making new friends, and hates saying goodbye at the end of a book—but there are always more characters in her head, clamouring for attention until she can't wait to tell their stories.

Recent titles by the same author:

A FAMILY TO COME HOME TO
A VERY SPECIAL PROPOSAL
HER LONGED-FOR FAMILY*
HIS LONGED-FOR BABY*
HIS UNEXPECTED CHILD*

**The ffrench Doctors*

CHAPTER ONE

'SO, HAVE you hooked yourself a doctor, yet, Lil?' her sister Iris asked, but the question could just as well have been put by anyone of the noisy group gathered in her parents' cramped living room.

'I'm not *trying* to hook one. I don't need to because I'm a doctor myself,' Lily pointed out rationally, but that cut no ice with her family.

'A complete waste of time and money, that's what I call it,' her mother pronounced—as usual—as she heaved herself off 'her' corner of the settee to put the kettle on again. 'You've got more debts than your father and I have had our whole lives and you still can't find yourself a husband. By the time I was your age, I'd already had five children and there was another one on the way.'

Lily had heard that particular refrain so many times that it was easy to tune it out. Her mother wouldn't deliberately hurt any of her children, although her habit of speaking her mind had caused more than a few hidden bruises.

It was her sisters and sisters-in-law that she found it harder to deal with. Their pitying glances in her direction and their conversations were just quiet enough for them to pretend that she wasn't supposed to hear but loud enough that she was left in no doubt what they thought of the 'uppity cow' trying to pretend that she was so much better than they were.

She stifled a sigh when her father gave a pointed jerk of his head to tell her that, as the eldest, she should have followed her mother out of the room to help her get his meal. She couldn't remember the first time she'd done it. It had been so many years ago that it was hidden in the mists of time, along with the memory of the first time she'd spooned food into her younger siblings' mouths and changed their nappies.

Sometimes she wondered why she bothered coming home at all when it felt as if she had to spend the whole time apologising for who she was and the choices she'd made. Of course, she knew why she *did* come—because she loved her family, no matter what. It was just that sometimes she wished…

'Do you still remember how to peel potatoes, now that you can afford to eat out all the time?' demanded her mother, as she bustled around a kitchen that had hardly changed from the day Lily had been born. Appliances had been replaced as they had given out and the cupboards had been repainted, but the colour scheme was the same magnolia and white it had always been. It was ironic that tastes in interior decorating had turned full circle so that it was back in fashion again.

'Doctors don't have time to eat out all the time, even if they could afford it,' she said quietly, as she reached for the peeler and the first of a mountain of potatoes. 'As students, we're so short of money we can barely afford to eat and once we've qualified, we're left with massive debts to pay off, so we *still* can't afford it.'

'So where was the point in doing all that studying?' Rose Langley demanded impatiently. 'Your father started working shifts as soon as he left school but at least the two of us got time to see each other. You seem to do nothing but work, and men don't like it when a woman doesn't pay them any attention…' Lily saw her throw a sideways glance at her eldest's well-worn jeans and generic sweatshirt. 'Or when she doesn't make the effort to do herself up a bit.'

That jab hit a sensitive spot and Lily winced. In spite of her sisters' taunts that there was 'no point in gilding the Lily', it was still a fact that she was the plain one of the family, even if she had been the only one of the girls to inherit her father's long, lean build.

'Everything I wear is clean, bought and paid for,' she pointed out defensively. 'I have to dress smartly to meet the patients in the orthopaedic clinic but when I'm in the operating theatre I'm in cotton scrubs.'

'I've seen them on the telly. Totally shapeless green pyjamas,' her mother said, and tut-tutted with distaste. 'How is any man going to be attracted to you in that? Now, if you had a boob job, or something, to give you a bit of shape…' She shook her head wearily. 'I know. I know. You couldn't afford to even if you wanted to, but if you're ever going to get married and have a family you're going to have to buck your ideas up before all the good ones are gone. You're over thirty already.'

Her tone of voice made it sound like eighty and Lily supposed that to a woman who'd already had most of her family by that age, she'd even gone beyond being classed as a late starter. It was definitely time to redirect the conversation, and subtlety wasn't an option.

'Mum, I think *you* got the last really good one,' she said with blatant flattery, her tongue firmly in her cheek. 'How can I get married to someone who doesn't measure up to Dad?'

'Well, there is that, I suppose,' her mother agreed, with more than a touch of smugness. 'Your dad's never let me down in all the years we've been married. He brought his pay cheque home to me every week…until work started putting it straight into the bank for him. He's not a smoker or much of a drinker, not like most of his mates, nor does he chase around after other women.'

'He doesn't need to,' Lily pointed out, with a sly look at her mother to see how the sweet talk was going down. 'He got all the woman he needs when he got you.'

'Get on with you,' Rose said dismissively, but a coy grin lifted the corners of her mouth at Lily's implied compliment.

The deliberate innuendo had the desired effect of sidetracking her mother's perennial complaint, but the strange thing was, deep down Lily actually meant what she'd said. Her parents *were* well matched and totally content with their separate roles within their marriage, and her father was the sort of honest, hard-working man that was a million miles from the self-obsessed hustlers and chancers around today. Where had all the solid, reliable hard-working men gone…the ones who would make a commitment and stick to it through thick and thin? She certainly hadn't come across any…not that she was looking. She still had years of work before her debts were paid and she achieved the coveted position of consultant.

Now, if only someone would come up with an alternative

topic of conversation over the dinner table—something other than Lily Langley's many shortcomings—she might be able to return to her flat without indigestion.

She'd actually hoped that someone would have remembered that she was due to start her new job in the morning and that it was, hopefully, the last rung in her career ladder before she reached the very top.

Unfortunately, the inner workings of the hospital hierarchy couldn't be less interesting to this cheerful gathering, especially with a traditional roast dinner in front of them and at least half a dozen members of the next generation needing assistance to refuel for the next noisy round of hide and seek in the garden.

'Give me strength!' Razak pleaded with the oblivious walls of his flat then let loose with a string of curses in his native language. He knew he was not very good at waiting around when something needed doing, and the interminable delay while committees talked something to death was driving him crazy.

'When are they *ever* going to get off the fence and make a decision? It's been *weeks* since I outlined my plan, and the new surgeon starts tomorrow.'

It was bad enough that the problems with the foundations of the new building had set completion back by several weeks. He'd really hoped that he would have had an answer by now so he could have begun recruiting staff. It was important that everything should be up and running with as few glitches as possible. With everything ironed out before the new surgeon arrived they could have jumped straight into the new system, and he'd been waiting for the decision—the final decision?—all afternoon, knowing that the committee was due to meet today. But, then, he didn't know whether his proposal was even on the agenda.

He would have to look on the bright side and treat the aggravating delay as a chance to see the new member of his team at work. His plans called for a skilled surgeon who could combine work of the highest standard with a willingness to work hard and fast without direct supervision. He might need several sessions of observation before he would be confident about handing his patients over for closing. And all the while, at the back of his mind, was the fact that even if he did get the go-ahead, he didn't have long to find out whether the system worked. It wouldn't be long before he came to the end of his time here and he needed so much more experience before he'd be ready to take on the responsibility for setting up a whole new orthopaedic department.

'So, I can make best use of the delay, but if the committee doesn't make the right decision in the end, and *soon*...'

His railings were curtailed by the chirp of his mobile phone and he fished it out of his pocket. A glance at the number displayed on the screen had him smiling immediately.

'Hey, Karim! How are you, baby brother?'

'Not so much of the baby, thank you,' the voice on the other end growled in mock anger. 'You should show me more respect, even if you are some big important doctor. It won't be long before you have to make obeisance...' He cut himself off with a curse of his own. 'I'm sorry about that. It was thoughtless in the circumstances when the honour is yours by right and will only be passed on when our father is...with us no more. It's just...'

'Forget it, Karim. That sort of jest is part of the way we

relate to each other and has nothing to do with being impatient for someone to die so you can step into their shoes,' Razak finished for him, sparing his brother's blushes at such a *faux pas*. 'Don't worry about it. I know you weren't being disrespectful but...how are they?'

'Much the same as usual,' Karim reported cautiously. 'Physically, they're far frailer than they'd ever admit, but mentally as sharp as ever. And your mother is forever begging your father to order you to return home so she can persuade you to change your mind about the succession. She still expects to put on a lavish wedding when you return. Dita will have taken all her exams by then.'

Razak's antennae went up when he heard the change in Karim's voice when he'd mentioned Dita's name. Could it be that the girl he'd been betrothed to almost from the cradle had grown up into the sort of woman who would catch Karim's eye?

Unfortunately, to Razak she could never be anything other than an extra sister—there had never been that extra spark between them. That was one of the reasons why he'd been so willing to help Dita fight for permission to travel abroad to study. With her horizons widened, she would be far less likely to allow her parents to browbeat her into a marriage that neither of the participants wanted.

And if Karim were to take her eye...?

'How is the project coming on?' Razak demanded briskly, turning his mind away from the more frivolous side of life. He had goals to achieve before he could even think about taking a mate. 'Will everything be finished by the time I return?'

'Of course,' Karim said confidently. 'By the time my brother the eminent consultant orthopaedic surgeon returns to his homeland, there will be a brand-new, fully equipped orthopaedic centre ready and waiting for him. Don't forget, it is Karim the Organiser managing this project, so all will be well.'

They bantered for several minutes before Razak remembered that he was still hoping that he would get that all-important phone call from his present hospital.

'I must go,' he said with a pang of homesickness. It had been so many years since he'd made anything more than a cursory visit there, but in a matter of months he would return for good. 'You will let me know if…if they need me to come back sooner?'

'Of course, big brother,' Karim reassured him quietly. 'I won't let you down. Go with God.'

Razak sighed heavily and sank back into the comfort of his recliner when the connection was broken. Sometimes he felt really guilty for being so far away when his parents were growing so frail. Not that he would be allowed to take care of their health even if he were right on the spot. His mother was far too traditional to be comfortable with a male doctor and his father would always see him as a little boy and consequently ignore any advice he gave him.

'A thirty-one-year-old boy,' he scoffed aloud even as he shot back his cuff for another glare at his watch, then gave a growl of annoyance when he realised that he wouldn't be getting any answers today. 'At this rate, I'll already have finished my contract and returned home by the time they make their minds up.'

For a moment he contemplated staying where he was to watch some mindless pap on the television, but the idea didn't appeal. He seemed to have spent most of the day sitting down and felt a desperate need for some exercise.

'A gallop on horseback,' he said longingly, remembering the muscular feel of the back of the horse between his thighs and the hot wind streaming through his hair the last time he'd been home. But this was neither the time nor the place. The only horse suited to a city street certainly wasn't the sort of beast he was happy riding. His tastes ran to pure-blooded Arabians, hardy, strong far beyond their refined appearance, more intelligent than any dog and with an intrinsic fire that was bred bone-deep in them.

'That's the first thing I'll do the next time I go home,' he promised himself. 'I shall take a horse out and lose myself for a day, so I can refresh my soul.' But in the meantime he had a choice of running round and round on the indoor track at his sports club or swimming endless lengths in the pool, and he could make that decision when he got there. Then it would be time to sleep if he was going to be refreshed enough to deal with the fresh blood coming into the department in the morning.

'Dr L. Langley,' he mused aloud, wondering what the L stood for. He'd been angry when he'd first heard that a female surgeon had been appointed to his team, believing that the more senior consultants in the department had done it deliberately to spoil his chances of making a success of his project. But as he was only here on a short contract, he'd been allowed no say in the decision and would have to hope that if she wasn't up to doing what he needed at the moment, she was at least willing to learn.

'Enough!' He hefted his sports bag over his shoulder and grabbed keys and phone, determined to switch his brain off to everything connected to work.

He would get to know all about Dr Langley soon enough.

Hoping that she was a dedicated surgeon with the power and stamina of a plough horse was definitely not politically correct, but he didn't need some delicate, willowy, model type who couldn't carry her share of the load, no matter how easy she might be on the eye.

'Women don't belong in orthopaedics,' said a voice behind the door, just as Lily began to push it open, and she froze in disbelief as it continued with all the authority of some demi-god pronouncing from on high. 'They just don't have the upper-body strength for it. If they want to do surgery, they should stick to something they're more suited to.'

For just a second she contemplated turning on her heel and retreating to the locker room, but retreat had never been her way. Otherwise she'd never have got so far in her chosen field. With her chin tilted just a fraction higher, she forced a smile to her face and took the last step that brought her denigrator into full view. 'So, while most of the one and a half thousand orthopaedic surgeons in the country are running waiting lists of up to a hundred and forty patients, each waiting for up to nine months for their operation, you're suggesting that I should spend my time doing tummy tucks instead?' she said, while inside her head she was groaning, *Not again!*

She'd hoped that, having got this far, she would at least have proved to the 'old school' orthopaedic surgeons that she was capable of doing the job, but it seemed as if their prejudices were still alive and festering unchecked in her new job. Did her immediate boss feel the same way?

Of the all-male group that had turned to face her, it was

easy to spot the one looking uncomfortable at being overheard and he was the one she strode towards first with her hand outstretched. She took a grim delight in demonstrating that he was nearly a head shorter than she was and he was also definitely past his prime, with a large gut filling out his theatre greens like an advanced pregnancy.

'I'm Lily Langley,' she announced, probably completely unnecessarily as they'd just been discussing her appointment. Well, she mused as she deliberately made a point of offering her hand to each in turn, forcing them to introduce themselves, there was one good point about that embarrassing start—at least she hadn't been left in any doubt about their attitude towards her.

One, Colin Wetherall, even went so far as to try to crush her knuckles under the guise of shaking her hand but *he* was the one left wincing, the hours she'd spent in the gym finally paying off in spades.

Not that she'd hurt him, she reassured herself silently as she worked her way around the semi-circle. She'd only flexed her hard-won muscles enough to let him know that his attempt at a power play hadn't worked. Then she turned to face the final member of the group.

'Hello,' she said, as she actually had to look up a couple of inches to meet eyes so dark that with the light behind him it was almost impossible to see where pupil and iris met. But it was the twinkle of humour in them that robbed her of words.

'Razak Khaled Khan,' he said, the harsh syllables of his name softened by a voice that flowed like honey over her nerves, then he held out his hand, lowering his voice as he added, 'Be gentle with me, please!'

Lily laughed aloud. She couldn't help it when he'd

managed to tickle her sense of the ridiculous. She wouldn't even attempt to intimidate someone like this, especially when he was her boss.

He had such innate presence that she didn't know how she'd managed to miss seeing him immediately when she'd walked into the room, but now that she'd met his eyes, it seemed impossible to look away.

'Not all of us feel the same way as Reg and Colin,' he reassured her. 'Some of us have actually learned that it's not just *what* we do but *how* we do it that matters.'

'Thus proving evolutionary theory correct?' she queried, suddenly realising that her hand was still securely wrapped in his and tugging surreptitiously. To her surprise, he resisted, tightening his grip fractionally to prevent her retrieving it.

He tightened his grip still further and nodded when she automatically matched the pressure with her own. 'Good. You have worked hard to improve your strength, but have you sacrificed dexterity?' he challenged.

'I can thread a needle with the best of them,' she reassured him. 'But you'll see for yourself when we start work.'

'Not if *he* has his way,' interrupted Reg with an unexpected touch of venom to his tone. 'He's been trying to get the hospital to agree to some ridiculous conveyor-belt system that will mean we wouldn't even have time to breathe, let alone speak, and as for mentoring… Forget it! Thank goodness the hospital's administrators have got more sense than wasting scarce resources on it.'

Lily saw the way Razak's face fell with disappointment and she felt an unexpected pang of sympathy. Whatever this scheme was, it was clearly close to his heart.

'They have sent the department a written decision?' he

demanded, turning on his heel to stride towards the pigeon-holes on the wall behind the door, then flicking impatiently through the handful of items waiting in the slot labelled 'Khan'.

'Well, no,' Reg admitted reluctantly. 'But it stands to reason that they will, man. It's taken years to get the funding released for that new theatre suite to be built. Do you really think they're going to hand the whole thing over to a surgeon who's only going to be here for a few months, just so he can waste time, effort and precious resources trying to prove an...an alcohol-fuelled brainwave?'

'I don't drink alcohol,' her new boss said with admirable restraint. 'And I would have thought you would jump at the chance to have someone else working in the new theatres. Then he could suffer while all the teething problems are sorted out.

'Anyway.' He turned to face Lily and his sombre expression was immediately lightened by a smile. 'It is time to give you the guided tour, Dr Langley. You will need to know your way around the rest of the hospital in case we get a call from A and E, and also to know where everything is within the department in case they send something urgent up to Theatre.'

'Actually, I had a tour when I came for my interview,' she reminded him, conscious that his time must be too precious to act as a glorified tour guide. 'The one bit they couldn't show me was the new operating suite because it was still a building site. Is it really nearly finished?'

'Do you want to see?' he offered, with all the enthusiasm of a puppy dropping a ball at her feet in the hope that she would want to play.

'Of course.' She grinned, then was glad of her long legs when she had to quicken her pace to keep up with him when he strode out of the room and set off down the corridor.

'Oh, I am so sorry,' he apologised a moment later, coming to a sudden halt so that she almost ploughed into his back.

'For what?' She tried to appear unaffected in spite of the fact that her pulse had just accelerated from sixty to a hundred and twenty beats with his unexpected proximity.

She was close enough to feel the heat emanating from his lean body through the cream-coloured shirt he wore, close enough, even, to be able to see the beginning of a tangle of dark hairs at the unbuttoned throat of that shirt.

Suddenly she was uncomfortably aware that she knew something as intimate as the fact that her new boss had hair on his chest, and Lily felt the beginning of a blush warming her cheeks.

He was staring in amazement when he found that she was right behind him, those dark eyes dropping the length of her long trouser-clad legs with a dawning smile. 'I was going to apologise for expecting you to be able to walk as fast as I do and rudely leaving you behind. This is the first time…the first time in my *life*…that a woman has been able to match my pace without running or getting out of breath.'

'So you're accustomed to having short-legged women running after you?' she quipped, then sucked in a sharp breath when she realised that she was actually flirting with the man. She'd never realised before that she even knew *how* to flirt.

The gleam in his eyes grew more pronounced and his teeth were startlingly white against his olive skin. 'Some of us have that cross to bear,' he admitted with mock modesty.

'And doubtless your long legs have been very useful to you as you leave your many suitors in your dust.'

Many suitors! Hah!

Lily knew what she looked like. She saw herself in the mirror every morning as she brushed her teeth and pulled her hair back into a no-nonsense twist. Even on a good day, she wouldn't stop traffic, unlike her sisters who had inherited their mother's better-endowed shape. So, was he mocking her for her lack of feminine attributes, his own subtle way of putting her down?

'I am sorry. Did I say something wrong?' He had obviously noticed her rapid change of expression as his broad forehead was pleated into a frown. 'If I have upset you…'

'No, no. Everything's fine,' she said hastily, averting her face from his intense scrutiny to look along the corridor. 'So, does this lead directly to the new operating suite?'

For just a moment she held her breath, certain that he was going to pursue the point, then released it in a silent sigh of relief when he began walking again.

'Nothing in this hospital leads directly to anything else,' he said wryly. 'I hope you have a good sense of direction.'

'If I get lost, you'll have to send out search parties,' she suggested, trying to recapture the light-hearted tone of their earlier conversation, but when Razak shouldered his way through the next set of swing doors she came to a sudden halt.

'Wow!' she breathed, feeling her eyes grow wider and wider as she looked around at the reception area for the new suite. 'This is bigger than my whole flat…well, it's more of a bedsit, really, but…' She shut her mouth, suddenly aware that she was babbling. That would have been bad enough if it was only in front of her new boss, but to have half a dozen workmen listening in, too…

'So, you like it?' he asked, as he beckoned her forward to point out the eventual purpose of each of the rooms, from the lowliest store cupboard to the two spacious theatres. 'They finished putting in the last of the flooring on Friday so they were given the weekend without any traffic on them to allow the adhesives to set properly. Today, as you can see, everywhere is being decorated.'

'But there are no doors to any of the rooms,' she said, suddenly realising why everywhere looked so strangely open.

'There will be doors,' he reassured her with a laugh. 'Apparently, they won't go in until all the equipment has been installed because otherwise they get in the way and can get damaged.'

'That's logical,' she agreed, 'especially as so many of them will be on automatic closing mechanisms. And you're hoping that we'll be moving in here when it's completed?'

'I'm lobbying hard,' he admitted as he led the way back out into the original part of the hospital. 'I don't know who you spoke to when you came for your interview, but did they tell you what I've been trying to organise in this new suite?'

'No one said a thing, other than that I would be working with a surgeon who wasn't staying very long and would that affect my acceptance of the post if I were offered it.'

'And you had no objection?'

'Not if it gave me the chance at a post here,' she said bluntly. 'The high standards of orthopaedic surgery in this hospital made it an obvious choice for the next step up the career ladder.'

'So, you are a career woman, then,' he said with a thoughtful frown as he paused in front of the door with his name across it. 'Have you no wish for a husband and children?'

'Certainly not for the foreseeable future,' she said firmly, wondering if his background led him to believe, like her family, that women belonged in the home, rearing children and catering to their husbands. 'I have worked far too hard to get this far to give it all up for nappies and midnight feeds. There is another rung I want to climb on the ladder first.'

'Well, let us see if we can make the next few months the perfect preparation for that goal,' he suggested as he led the way into his office. 'There is much to be done with so many patients waiting months in agony for their turn on the table, and this afternoon we have a clinic to determine the suitability of the next group to take their place. Come, I will show you their files.'

A tiny secret place inside Lily was actually disappointed that Razak had switched to a totally professional tone, completely devoid of any of the previous light-heartedness. The rest of her applauded it, knowing that the more experience she could gain by his side, the better it would be for her career.

After all, she rationalised, her career was more important to her than being friendly with the man who would help to hone her skills.

CHAPTER TWO

BY THE time she staggered back to her bedsit that evening Lily was totally exhausted and wondering if she was ever going to be able to keep up with Razak's seemingly inexhaustible supply of energy.

Things had started off calmly enough as the two of them had first examined an apparently endless series of patients referred by their GPs, many of them needing orthopaedic surgery sooner rather than later for their painful joints. Later that afternoon they had moved on to the review of the two patients who had been admitted that day for surgery the following morning, but before they had been able to take any sort of a break for her to ask any of the questions already buzzing around in her head, Razak had been contacted for an urgent consultation on a patient in the emergency department and she had found herself running in his wake when he had suggested she come, too.

'Sir, listen to this,' exulted a very young doctor as he reached out towards the blood-spattered body on the trolley in front of him. 'You can actually hear the bones grating when you spring the man's hips.'

'Don't!' snapped Razak, before he could make contact,

the word like the crack of a lash. 'How many times have you already done that?'

'A couple,' he admitted, then smiled almost innocently. 'It's the first time I've actually heard a break when I've done it and I—'

'And you could be responsible for killing the man,' Razak interrupted fiercely. 'What's his blood pressure doing? If the sharp edges of the broken bones damages one of the pelvic arteries he could bleed out in a matter of minutes. Your job here is to stabilise his condition so we can get him up to Theatre, yes?'

'Yes, sir,' he agreed, clearly crestfallen. 'Do you want to use an external fixator before he's transferred?'

'Have X-rays been taken yet to show the position of the fracture?' Razak demanded briskly. 'If there's more than one break we may have to. Otherwise, if you can guarantee not to make him any worse while he's transported to Theatre, we'll do it upstairs while we do an open reduction and internal fixation.'

Even as he was speaking, the radiographer was positioning the equipment above the moaning patient and there were so many members of staff noisily occupied in taking care of him that Lily wondered for a moment whether they would even hear the radiographer's warning countdown to the first exposure.

At the last second the last nurse whipped her hands off the body and stepped back smartly, only to step forward just as swiftly as soon as that view had been taken.

The whole process had to be repeated several times to build up an accurate picture of what was going on inside, and all the while the members of the resus team were going about their tasks. Machines were monitoring the patient's blood pressure and airway but one of the nurses was specifically detailed to document each dose of painkilling drug and every procedure as it was done while another was keeping up a soothing running commentary in the hope that it would make everything just a little less frightening.

At least the hospital had the latest digital X-ray technology, so there was no long wait while old-fashioned plates were hurried away to be developed. With this state-of-the-art equipment, as soon as the shot was taken it was available for viewing on the monitor with the touch of a button.

Razak muttered something vehement under his breath when he saw the first view, and even without knowing his language Lily could tell that he'd sworn. She certainly felt like it when she saw the damage the man had sustained.

'Definitely an external fixator,' she murmured as she stepped aside to reach for the wall phone. 'Who should I ask for to bring the kit down?'

'Can you see if Colin Wetherall's free at the moment?' Razak asked. 'Tell him what we've got here and that I'd like him to do a demonstration for you.'

'A demonstration?' she murmured under her breath, while someone up in the orthopaedic department checked to see if Colin was still in Theatre. He'd had two operations scheduled that afternoon, a knee and a shoulder. If everything had gone well, he should be nearly finished. But why should she need Colin to demonstrate the fixator kit? It wasn't as if she hadn't used it before, although, admittedly, not very often.

Was calling him down Razak's way of saying that he wasn't impressed with her level of skill? She didn't think she'd made any mistakes today, their only disagreements having been over matters of personal preference for various prosthetics.

'I hope he *is* free,' Razak said suddenly, his voice right behind her telling her that he'd come far closer than she'd realised. 'He spent some time in Russia at the institute where this particular fixator system was developed and he's nothing short of brilliant with it. The best in the department, I think.'

Lily hadn't known the man long, but she had a feeling that Razak didn't give praise easily, so it was with an unexpected feeling of anticipation that she waited to see what would happen. For the moment, her role was more of a passive observer, but that could change at any moment.

To the uninitiated, the external fixator kit that arrived just before Colin might have been confused with a rather sophisticated construction toy with its various shiny rods and connectors, but in the hands of someone who had obviously been taught by masters how to use it best, it was a revelation.

Using the X-rays as a guide, Colin swiftly tightened the special screws into position in the bones then fitted the rods between them, tightening them only when the pelvis had been restored to the correct shape.

'How's his blood pressure?' Colin demanded, without even lifting his head from the last titanium rod, his movements swift and accurate, while Razak automatically braced the unstable pelvis for him.

'No sign of hypovolaemia so far, but blood is being cross-matched and sent up to Theatre.'

They sounded so calm, but those few words were a measure of the potentially deadly nature of this particular injury. There were so many veins and arteries in this area and this sort of bony injury was often accompanied by massive soft-tissue injury and a more than fifty per cent chance of dying of massive blood loss.

So far, their patient had been lucky. His blood pressure was holding fairly steady, indicating that there was no great dip in his blood volume. He also seemed to have avoided any apparent injuries to his kidneys, bladder or urethra as there was no sign of blood in his urine or on the ultrasound scan that had largely replaced the need for peritoneal lavage.

Now, with Colin straightening up from his completed task and the pelvis stable enough for the patient to make the journey up to Theatre safely, it was just a case of opening him up on the table and performing an internal fixation of each of the fractures. Only then would the bones have a chance of healing normally so that the patient could walk again.

'Do you want me to finish the job off?' Colin offered. He tried to sound diffident but Lily had the feeling that this was the sort of case he thrived on. She'd known other surgeons who found the never-ending stream of joint replacements stultifying, only really enjoying the adrenaline rush of repairing life-threatening traumatic injuries.

'Do you have enough theatre time left?' Razak asked. 'You've already been operating this afternoon.'

Lily knew what he was asking. Their standard sessions were three and a half hours and this wasn't going to be an easy job or a quick one. If Colin had already operated on two patients that afternoon…

'One of mine didn't make it into Theatre this afternoon, unfortunately. She had a CVI on the ward just after she took her pre-med. She's up in ICU now.'

'In which case, be my guest,' Razak said with a smile, standing aside as the trolley set off towards the bank of lifts. 'Call me if you need another hand on the screwdriver.'

Lily felt a tremendous sense of anticlimax as everyone dispersed, leaving just the nurses to gather up the debris and get the room cleaned and restocked for the next emergency. She'd honestly believed that Razak would be operating on the patient and had been gearing herself up for the probability that she would be in the theatre with him.

'Don't be impatient!' he teased, and she wondered with a jolt whether he was also a mind-reader. 'I promise you'll have your chance tomorrow morning. I'll be putting you through your paces then.'

The anticipation was different this time, a mixture of excitement that she would be doing what she loved and dread lest he find her skills lacking.

But even as she followed him out of A and E and shared a lift with him up to the orthopaedic department to retrieve her purse and keys, there were questions circling inside her head.

It was nothing that anyone had said…more what they hadn't said or, even worse, things that had been hinted at. If she was going to be able to give of her best when the two of them were working together tomorrow, she needed to clear the air, and the only way of doing that was to ask for an explanation.

Even then she hesitated and it wasn't until he had his hand out towards the door of his office that she spoke.

'I need to speak to you,' she blurted. 'I…I need to ask you some questions.'

'Now?' he asked, turning back to her with a weary smile, and she remembered suddenly that he'd had a late night repairing the damage after a fight outside a pub last night. 'Of course,' he said politely, but as he turned to lead the way into his office his stomach growled and her feelings of guilt were doubled.

'Have you eaten?' he asked, then shook his head. 'Stupid question! Of course you haven't because you've spent the whole day in my shadow. So, will you join me for a meal?'

'Oh, but…' She was already shaking her head, unaccustomed to such invitations, especially at short notice. And to be invited by her boss… 'We don't need to… We…we can talk tomorrow,' she suggested hurriedly, cursing her pale complexion when she felt the searing heat of a blush.

To her surprise, he seemed completely oblivious to her discomfort.

'We won't have time to talk tomorrow,' he said flatly, 'certainly not without Colin and Reg and who knows who else listening in to every word. And if you have questions, we need to get them answered to clear your mind for the morning. You'll need all your concentration in my theatre. Anyway,' he added, not giving her time to come up with a solid objection as he pulled his door shut again and the keypad lock clicked shut, 'we both need to eat, Dr Langley, and we could talk at the same time. Very efficient.'

What could she do but agree, in spite of her automatic reluctance to share a meal with him? Partly it had been the formal way he'd spoken to her as Dr Langley that had made her give in, but that didn't explain the strange emotions churning inside her.

She was attracted to the man, that's what it was, she realised as he ushered her into her seat in the little French restaurant in one of the side streets near the hospital. And it had taken her this long to recognise the feeling because it the first time it had happened to her like this.

But, then, Razak Khan was a rather exceptional man…charismatic, powerful, good-looking, courteous… there wasn't much she couldn't admire about him. But somehow she understood that this went deeper than a surface appreciation for a handsome successful man… This was…

Nothing, she told herself fiercely as she buried her nose in her menu. This was her boss and if she was ever going to make it up that final rung of the ladder, she was going to have to keep her concentration where it mattered—on the job.

'So, explain this big scheme to me,' she invited brightly, and had to hide a wince when she heard how air-headed she sounded.

'How much do you know?' he countered, then had to pause when the waiter arrived to take their order, clearly delighted when Razak switched into fluent French.

If she concentrated hard, Lily found she could actually follow what the two of them were saying, and it was evidence of yet another fascinating facet of the man that she'd love to explore. When had he learned French and why? Was it his native language or…

That is *not* why you're sitting here, she reminded herself sternly. He asked you a question and now he's waiting for a reply.

'How much do I know?' she said. 'Apart from the fact that Reg hates it, nothing at all.'

'Wasn't it explained at your interview?' he demanded, clearly surprised by her reply.

'No. Not that I can…' She paused, suddenly remembering the moment when one of the bean-counters had started to ask her something, only to be talked down by Reg. Had that been the point when she should have found out what Razak was proposing to do? Had that been the moment when Reg had decided that appointing one of the women he so blatantly despised might be the straw that broke the camel's back as far as Razak's scheme went?

The more she thought about it, the more likely it seemed.

Without a strong, committed junior on his team…one with the stamina to keep up the pace for long hours at a stretch…the scheme would never get approval, never mind be a success.

A sudden sickening idea burst into her brain. Was *that* why she'd got the job in the first place? Not because she was the best candidate for the job but because Reg thought she would be a weak and feeble woman?

'What?' Razak demanded, breaking into her unpalatable thoughts.

'*What*, what?' she countered, wondering if he was waiting for an answer to another question. She honestly couldn't remember.

'I wanted to know if you'd reached a conclusion?' he asked patiently.

'A conclusion about what?' she temporised, hoping he would tell her which part of their conversation she'd missed.

'Well, you obviously had some sort of an internal debate going on just then, and from the expressions on your face I would guess that there *was* something said at your interview, but that someone—either Colin or Reg, but most likely Reg—prevented anyone telling you the whole story. So…' He frowned in concentration, far too close to the truth for her comfort. He really did seem to be able to read her thoughts. 'You were wondering why he didn't want you to know. After all, it would strengthen his case to have good surgeons withdrawing their candidacy for the job because they didn't like what they were being asked to do… No! That's not it!' he contradicted himself with a closer look at her face, as though the words were actually written there. 'You were wondering whether the reason you were offered the job was because the appointment of a woman as my junior would make it less likely that the scheme would be given the go-ahead. You were wondering whether you got the job because you were the weakest candidate rather than the strongest. Am I right?'

'Spot on,' she agreed through gritted teeth, steam practically coming out of her ears. 'Just wait till I tell that pompous—'

'Hey, don't get mad, get even!' he suggested, with a wicked grin that made his teeth seem even whiter in the darkened intimacy of their corner of the room.

'How?' she demanded, the thought definitely appealing.

'Prove him wrong,' he said simply. 'Be everything you can be so that he has to eat his words not just about women as orthopaedic surgeons but also about the scheme I'm trying to get going.'

'And about which I still have no idea,' she pointed out, and it was like letting loose a tidal wave of enthusiasm.

'It's a whole new way of managing lists for orthopaedic surgery,' he said with all the fervour of an evangelist, barely pausing to sample his meal when it arrived. 'Not new in America, where some surgeons have been doing it for years, or in France, where they also use a similar system, but as far as Britain is concerned…'

'Mr Khan?' she interrupted with a touch of impatience.

'Yes?' his own impatience was even greater for having been halted in mid-flow.

'What system are you talking about?'

'Oh! Yes!' He threw her a brilliant smile. 'I forgot to start at the beginning, didn't I?'

'Yes, you did, Mr Khan,' she agreed, for the first time feeling like smiling back.

'In that case, I apologise, Dr Langley, but I—'

'Lily,' she offered, before he could go any further. 'My name is Lily.'

'Lily,' he echoed thoughtfully, tilting his head on one side before shaking it. 'No, that's not the flower I was thinking of. I would have said jasmine.'

He'd actually been thinking about her name or…

'I'm wearing jasmine,' she blurted, wishing she'd kept her mouth shut when she realised she would have to explain. 'My mother's called Rose and she named us girls after flowers, too…Lily, Iris, Violet and Marguerite…and for years she's given us flower-scented toiletries for Christmas and birthday presents. This year mine was—'

'Jasmine,' he finished for her, then shocked her to the core by taking her hand in his and bringing her wrist up to his nose. 'No, nothing there,' he pronounced, almost seeming disappointed.

'Too much hand-washing,' she suggested, to cover the shiver of response that travelled the length of her spine when his dark eyes almost seemed to take inventory of the other places he might search out to find the elusive scent.

'Ah…you were saying?' she fumbled as she tugged to retrieve her hand, horrified by how swiftly things had strayed away from the purely businesslike. 'About the new system?'

she prompted, as she knotted both hands together on her lap, trying to quell the strange tingle that lingered where his fingers had held hers.

'Ah…yes.' She saw him blink as though it took an effort to gather his concentration. 'It's production-line surgery, to put it at its crudest. Have you heard anything about it?'

'Where the surgeon has a whole string of operating theatres on the go at one time, with juniors starting and closing the operations while the consultant does the complicated bit in the middle? Yes, I've heard of it,' she agreed with a buzz of excitement. 'Is it true that some can keep twelve theatres busy at once?'

'I believe so, although I didn't witness it when I was over in the States, or when I was in France, where orthopaedic surgeons use a version of the same system.'

'So what are the advantages over what happens here? Doesn't it tie up an enormous number of other staff—anaesthetists, nurses and so on? And then there's the number of specialist staff for post-operative care, too…and physiotherapists for mobilisation…and the number of beds needed all at once and…'

'I know! I know! These are all the objections that Reg has been pointing out *ad nauseam* to anyone who will listen, even though I have told him that I only want to use two theatres and to operate for five hours instead of three and a half.'

'So tell me about the benefits,' she challenged.

'For the hospital accountants, the first one is obvious,' he said with a shrug. 'The most expensive member of an operating team is the surgeon, and at the moment the hospital is paying for him…or her…to spend unnecessary time sitting drinking tea or coffee while they wait for the theatre to be cleared and restocked and their next patient to be prepped. It just doesn't make economic sense to pay them to be idle.'

'And secondly?' she prompted, already seeing that he'd thought deeply about this, having seen the system working in other countries.

'The benefit to the patients is when the waiting lists are cut to nothing,' he said decisively. 'Other countries are horrified by the idea that someone already in pain and needing replacement surgery for a hip, maybe, should then be put on a list and have to wait for up to nine months before their pain can be relieved. For some, the only bearable option is to pay to go privately, but for many, even that option is not possible because of the high costs involved. This just doesn't happen in France, for example, because the production-line system means that the theatres and surgeons are utilised properly…to full capacity.'

'And the disadvantages?'

'Once again, financial, with the cost of building and equipping extra theatres, and then there's the specialist theatre and ancillary staff. There's also the fact that if the waiting lists disappear, far fewer people will be interested in paying for their operations privately, so the surgeons who are boosting their incomes with private work will feel the pinch, apart from having to work longer shifts and work harder during the hours they're on shift.'

'So it's no wonder that Reg and his coterie are less than enthusiastic about your plans,' Lily said with dawning comprehension. 'If they agree with you, it's tantamount to upping their workload by nearly fifty per cent while dropping their income by a similar amount.'

'Don't forget the fact that their tea-breaks will virtually

disappear!' he added, then gave a sigh. 'It all just so frustrating when the theatre suite is all but completed and I've already got the anaesthetists and theatre staff on board.'

'So,' Lily mused thoughtfully, 'the last thing you needed was to have a female surgeon foisted on you. I suppose you see me as the last nail in the coffin of your plans.'

'To be honest, I won't know that until I see you work,' he said bluntly, those dark eyes fixing her steadily, unequivocally. 'If you're a good surgeon, you could actually be the card that wins the game.'

'So, before you start pushing them for the go-ahead, you need to know that Reg appointed the right person in spite of himself. I take it that when we're in Theatre together tomorrow morning, you'll be watching me like a hawk?'

'Will that worry you?' One dark brow lifted quizzically but there was a watchful stillness about the man that sent an atavistic shiver through her.

That was enough to put some steel into her spine. She'd never allowed any man to intimidate her and wasn't about to now.

'Not in the least,' she said firmly, confident of her abilities. 'I might not have had the experience you have, but I'm good at what I do. Very good, because I've worked hard at it.'

There was an unexpected warmth and...was it respect?... in his eyes. 'I'm looking forward to it,' he said softly.

If ever there was a challenge to put her on her mettle, Razak Khan was that challenge, she thought as they finished their meal, tacitly agreeing to stick to more general topics as they got the measure of each other.

It was only when he'd walked her back to the hospital and she was making her solitary way towards her cramped bedsit that she remembered her idea of having a word with the chairman of the committee, just in case Reg *had* read the bean-counters right.

Initiating this new scheme *was* going to use up finite resources, with a full staff on duty in both theatres simultaneously, but if Razak had the support of *everyone* on those teams, even his untried junior… If everyone knew that she was fully behind Razak's initiative, would that remove any of their reservations?

Of course, much of that would largely depend on how well she performed the next day, whether she and her new boss could find that elusive synchronicity that made for a good operating team, and if she was too tired, it definitely wouldn't happen.

Razak flung the bedcovers to the floor in a fit of impatience and swore softly into the darkness.

'What on earth is wrong with me?' he demanded aloud. 'So what if she's a woman? She's an orthopaedic surgeon, and that's what matters.'

Except she wasn't like any other orthopaedic surgeon he'd ever met. He'd never met anyone who presented such a calm, serene exterior while underneath… Did she even know the depth of passion that was hidden under the surface? He doubted it. There was such an *untouched* air about her that it aroused the hunter in him the way no woman ever had.

She didn't even look like any of the other women in his life. His upbringing had conditioned him to appreciate the lush voluptuous woman who knew how to pleasure a man, while Lily…

She was so much like her name…tall, slender, elegant,

cool, with her pale gold hair and even paler skin the colour of rich cream sprinkled with just a handful of cinnamon freckles. For a crazy moment he found himself speculating whether those sun-kissed spots were confined to her face and arms or whether they extended to the rest of her body. He was seized with the urge to explore beneath the camouflage of her neat professional clothes to find…

'No!' he growled, and winced when he heard the throaty tones of arousal in his voice. Was she some kind of witch that she'd tied his thoughts up in her, his body already in thrall?

It couldn't be allowed, not if he was going to achieve his goal. He must be allowed to set up this programme if he was going to strengthen his claim in time for his return to his homeland. There were so many willing to point the finger and to whisper of nepotism. This was important to him. This was one thing that he needed to achieve on merit alone. He was so close to achieving his dream that he could almost touch it, and he couldn't allow anything—or anyone—to stand in his way.

'So, tomorrow you will watch Lily as she operates and you will do it with eyes as sharp as the scalpel in her hand,' he told himself sternly. 'You will assess her skills and her weaknesses and you will decide whether she is going to be an asset or…'

He shook his head. There could be no *or*. Failure was not an option. Lily Langley was his junior, for better or worse, and if he needed to retrain her himself in time for the start of the project, he would do it.

'I just hope you're up to it, pretty Lily,' he growled. 'If not, the next few months could be misery for both of us.'

CHAPTER THREE

Lily deliberately arrived early the next morning, nearly an hour before her shift was due to start, with a squadron of butterflies in her stomach.

She was determined to have one last check through the equipment she was going to be using for the first operation and wanted to do it before Razak arrived and began monitoring her every action, but she was too late. He was already there, as alert as if he always enjoyed a full eight hours' sleep a night, while she was so nervous that she felt as if she might fly apart at any second.

'Keen and eager?' he asked her, as he strode along beside her towards the theatre they'd been allocated that morning, but she was certain that somehow he knew that it was nerves that had brought her in this early.

'Looking forward to getting on with the job,' she agreed, wishing she dared cross her fingers for luck. Although she had a feeling that luck wouldn't be enough to take her through this first operation. She was going to need to demonstrate every bit of the skills she'd learned so far, while learning everything she could from the man who had so much expertise to impart.

And the first thing she learned was a lesson in simple humanity.

Their patient had stuck in her mind from their meeting yesterday, soon after her admission to the orthopaedic ward.

Cicely Turner wasn't a very tall woman, and she weighed hardly more than a sparrow, which was probably the only reason why she'd managed to keep going as long as she had on hips that were so damaged it was a wonder she was still able to stand, let alone lead a full and active life with dozens of grandchildren and children around her.

'My mother's hip replacement was a success but my father's was a disaster,' she'd told them bluntly when the two of them had invited her into Razak's office to review her case notes, the X-rays prominently displayed on a view box. The whole procedure had then been discussed with her in detail before she had been asked whether she had any questions.

'Not really, no, thank you very much,' she'd said politely. 'I'm certainly not expecting to be able to run a marathon when you've done it. I just want you to promise me that you'll take the pain away so I can help my children out by doing a bit of babysitting now and again. I do love getting my hands on the babies,' she confided in an aside to Lily. 'Luckily, by the time I couldn't have any more of my own, my children had started producing their own, so I've always had plenty to cuddle.'

Razak had pointed out, quite properly, that he couldn't guarantee the success of any operation. 'All I can guarantee is that we'll both do our very best,' he'd said seriously.

And that morning, before the anaesthetist had put her under, he'd made a point of going through to hold her hand and tell her that he hadn't forgotten his promise.

The smile of relief on the woman's face wasn't something that Lily would forget in a hurry, neither was the fact that Razak had understood just how frightened Cicely would be in such an alien situation. It was proof of something special in the man that, despite the time constraints on their limited theatre hours, he had sacrificed a couple of those precious minutes to put her at ease.

The operation itself was textbook perfect, as was the meshing of their skills as the procedure unfolded.

The joint was badly worn, their first view of it once it had been disarticulated confirming Razak's diagnosis that this patient would be requiring a complete prosthetic replacement for both components of the ball-and-socket joint.

'I still think the Exeter will be the best choice for her,' Razak murmured, with another long look from the open joint in front of them to the most recent X-rays displayed on the wall.

'One of the earliest designs and still the best?' Lily suggested, wondering if he could tell that she was smiling behind her mask. 'I believe it got its name because the man who designed it worked at Exeter University in the engineering department.'

'That's probably why it has stood the test of time with so few modifications, then—because it was designed to stand up to the stresses to which it would be subjected, rather than to look pretty,' he commented, even as she saw him checking his measurements to ensure the finished leg length would match its opposite number.

It was strange how, as soon as she'd touched the scalpel to the woman's prepared flesh, all hint of nerves disappeared. She was still overwhelmingly aware of Razak standing just inches away from her as she dissected her way through the layers of skin and muscle but when his hands came into the operating field it wasn't as an intrusion into what she was doing but rather as if she'd somehow grown another pair of hands to help her to complete the task.

'Ready to close?' he asked, when the cement that had been specially developed to hold the prosthesis to the bone had set properly and the smooth new ball of the joint had been relocated in the relined socket. Lily had been concentrating so hard that it seemed that just moments had passed since the initial incision. A quick glance up at the clock hung prominently on the theatre wall showed that, in fact, the patient had been under anaesthetic for nearly three hours. 'Are you happy with everything?' Razak added, almost as an afterthought.

For just a second she wondered if the question was some sort of test and she began to doubt herself, but a quick inspection of the operating site told her that all was exactly how it should be.

'I'm happy,' she confirmed, and held out her hand for the first of the absorbable sutures that would be buried deep inside the muscles of the thigh.

Her technique was flawless, Razak mused as he stood aside to watch Lily closing the final layers of the wound with the neatest row of stitches he'd seen in a long time.

Her requests and comments to the other staff had been calm, clear and concise and her concentration…probably better than his own, he admitted with a wry smile behind his mask. Particularly today when his focus had continually been interrupted by an awareness of the soft floral scent that had drifted around him from her skin.

This strange sensitivity towards a work colleague had never happened to him before, even though he'd been surrounded by women in every operating theatre he'd worked in.

Was it just her perfume? That was unlikely. The human sensory system was designed to be able to switch off such input after a relatively short time.

So, was it Lily herself? It certainly seemed that way, although he had no idea what it was about the woman that was affecting him this way. There was something about her that was different to every other woman he'd known but…was she *that* different that she could interfere with his usual level of concentration?

He suddenly realised with a frown of concern that he might be in a different sort of trouble if his scheme didn't get the go-ahead.

At least with Lily working in the other theatre, prepping and closing each patient in turn, he wouldn't be working beside her. It might be the only way he'd be able to demonstrate that the scheme worked, and that was so important to him when he had much less than a year left before he returned to his own country at the end of his contract. After all, it was exactly this sort of system that he was hoping to instigate when he returned home and he needed a success here to silence any doubts.

And still he couldn't help watching her as she straightened up from applying the final wound dressing, taking in the way she ran a smoothing hand over the supportive anti-embolic stockings that Cicely had been helped into before the operation. They would be removed and replaced twice a day for skin inspection and hygiene purposes.

Then he saw her checking that the notes specified the

correct doses of post-operative pain relief and that the antibiotic prophylaxis that had commenced preoperatively would continue until healing had taken place. The last thing any of them needed was for their patient to suffer a deep vein thrombosis or develop a post-operative infection that could destroy their work.

'Good,' he said quietly, when she finally stepped back and the trolley was wheeled through to the post-operative ward where Cicely's recovery from the anaesthetic would be closely monitored. 'That went very smoothly. I am pleased.'

He could see from the way her eyes lit up that she was smiling, even though her expression was still largely hidden behind her mask. He'd had years of discovering how much a man could learn about a woman when he could see little more than a pair of expressive eyes, but for the first time was discovering just how much physical effect they could have on him.

Out of the corner of his eye he saw her strip her blood-stained gloves off, the way she automatically tucked one inside the other without having to watch her hands performing the manoeuvre a testament to just how many times she'd done it. Her aim into the bin was equally accurate.

Only then did she pull her mask down around her throat to show him that her smile was every bit as wide and just as delighted as he'd imagined.

'Really? You're pleased with the way I...it...?' She stumbled to a halt, an endearing hint of pink darkening that creamy skin. He took pity on her.

'Yes, I was pleased with the way the operation went and, yes, I was most definitely pleased with your technique,' he said firmly. 'Now, let's get out of here so the staff can get everything ready so we can do it all over again.'

He gestured for her to precede him out of the room, ironically looking forward for the first time to wasting some of their precious theatre time drinking tea with her and rehashing the recently completed procedure.

It was only as she strode ahead of him and his eyes slid down the long slender length of her legs that he noticed that where other theatre staff had written their names or initials on the clogs they wore in Theatre, Lily had drawn a simple stylised picture of the flower she had been named after. The unexpected touch of whimsy suddenly made him realise that there could be far more to this woman than the fact that she was a talented junior surgeon.

The second procedure, a debridement and removal of osteophytes from an osteoarthritic knee, went every bit as smoothly as the first and his heart lifted with the realisation that, whether he had intended it or not, Reg had certainly chosen a perfectionist to be his junior.

His only lingering concern as they reached the end of their shift was whether someone so slender would have the stamina to keep up that standard over the longer operating sessions he wanted to instigate, and neither of them would know the answer unless or until they were given a chance to find out.

'Dr Langley. A word, please,' Reg Smythe said pompously as she was just about to leave the orthopaedic department at the end of her shift.

Lily glanced swiftly at her watch, delighted to see that she really didn't have time to find out what he wanted to say. She had a strong feeling that he wouldn't have used the same unpleasantly autocratic tone if she'd been a man and her respect for the head of department took a further dip.

'I'm sorry, Mr Smythe, but I'm going to be late for an appointment.'

'An appointment?' he echoed superciliously, as though *nothing* could be more important than his request.

Lily didn't want to give the man any more excuses to dislike her. 'With someone in the administration department,' she added helpfully.

'The administration department?' he repeated impatiently.

'That's where they sort out contracts and tax codes and things, isn't it?' Lily elaborated blandly. She certainly didn't want to give him a hint that it was the senior administrator's office that was her destination. It would be better if he didn't know what she hoped to accomplish that evening.

'Ah, yes. Probably,' he said dismissively. 'I suppose you'd better run along, then. I'll have a word with you later.'

Not if I see you first, she said to herself as she hurried away from him, hoping she didn't look half as guilty as she felt, but until she knew what the chairman of the committee wanted to talk about, she wasn't going to risk any conversation with Razak's nemesis. For all she knew, the man who was one of the hospital's most senior administrators *did* want to talk to her about her tax code or her pay scale, unlikely though that might be for a man of his status. His message had given her no reason to think that it could be anything to do with the proposed change in operating methods.

That didn't mean that she hadn't been speculating wildly ever since she'd taken the phone call from his secretary, and her pulse was pounding at almost twice its normal rate by the time she was shown into his office.

'Dr Langley!' he said cheerfully, doing her the courtesy

of standing up as she entered the room and coming round from behind his desk to offer his hand. 'Thank you for being so prompt. I know how difficult it can be, with unexpected delays in procedures in Theatre. Do make yourself comfortable. Can I offer you something to drink? Tea? Coffee?'

'No… Thank you for the offer, but I'll be having a meal when I get home,' she added hurriedly when her need to find out what all this was about nearly made her forget her own manners.

'And how has your first day in Theatre gone?' he asked, as soon as they were both settled into the plush leather chairs grouped round a glass-topped table at the other end of his office. 'Any problems?'

For just a second Lily was tempted to groan aloud. Obviously he was a man who liked to work his way around to a topic rather than coming straight to the point. She was going to have to be patient.

'No problems at all, thank you,' she said as politely as a recent graduate of a ladies' finishing school. 'In fact, I thoroughly enjoyed it.'

'Good. Good. Excellent,' he murmured with a benign smile, then fell silent for several excruciatingly long seconds before starting again. 'I suppose Mr Khan has had time to tell you all about the radical new operating scheme he's proposed?'

'Do you really think it's so radical, sir?' she questioned, suddenly impatient. 'It's certainly different to the usual way of organising things here—and in most hospitals in this country—but with the advances in technology meaning that more patients are suitable for surgery than ever before, the old ways are never going to be able to keep up with the number of people needing operations. It makes perfect sense to me that we would need to update the rather leisurely way we organise our operating methods in response to the needs of those patients.'

'Leisurely?' he repeated with a slightly stunned look on his face, and she wondered if she'd gone too far. After all, she still didn't know exactly what he wanted from her...why he'd asked for this meeting in the first place. So, even though there was plenty more she *could* say, she refused to be drawn any further until she knew what was going on. Now was obviously the time to wait him out until he chose to continue.

'So,' he said finally after a silence that seemed to stretch for ever, 'am I to take it that—should Mr Khan's scheme be approved—you would be willing to work as his junior in the second of the new theatres?'

'Not to put too fine a point on it, but I'd leap at the chance, sir,' Lily said honestly. 'I know I've only worked with him for two operations today, but that was enough to tell me that he's exceptionally talented.' A sudden thought crossed her mind. 'Of course, it would also depend on whether *he* was willing to have me opening and closing for him.'

Ian Eardle startled her by laughing aloud. 'Oh, I don't think there's any worry about that,' he said. 'Almost as soon as he came out of Theatre the man was in here confirming that, whether Mr Smythe had intended it or not, the perfect person had been appointed for the post. It sounds as if the two of you have the start of a mutual admiration society.'

The thought that Razak had made a point of voicing his approval of her skills sent a heady warmth flooding through her. Maybe that was why she forgot herself long enough to overstep the bounds of discretion to blurt out eagerly, 'So, will Razak...Mr Khan...be getting the go-ahead to start the new scheme as soon as the new theatre suite is finished? He really needs to know as soon as possible so he can begin to get everything organised. For a start, it will mean contacting patients to let them know that their operations are being brought forward, and then there are all the staff who need to know that their hours will be different as soon as the five-hour operating shifts start, *and* the surgical wards… Oh, I'm *so* sorry!' She stumbled to a halt, her face flaming when she realised just how she'd been gabbling on. 'I know it's none of my business, telling you—'

'Oh, don't apologise, my dear!' he interrupted with an unconcerned wave of his hand. 'It's wonderful to know that you're so enthusiastic about your work and aware of all the ramifications of the proposed changes.' He pursed his lips for a moment and tapped them with a thoughtful finger before finally shaking his head.

'Unfortunately, I can't give you an answer to your question yet. It wouldn't be appropriate, for a start, to give any decision to a junior member of a department before the seniors had been informed.'

He suddenly stood up and offered her his hand, the signal that their conversation was over, then leaned towards her and added conspiratorially, 'Unofficially, Dr Langley, if I were you, I'd make sure you get as much sleep as you can, while you can. I've a feeling that your life is about to get very busy, very soon.'

Lily couldn't wait to see Razak the next morning, desperate to find out if the decision had been formally announced.

She'd been almost too excited to sleep, in spite of their busy day, but when she'd contemplated calling the hospital switchboard to ask to be put in contact with him, she knew she was going too far.

Imagine what the hospital grapevine would make of *that* if it became common knowledge. It didn't bear thinking about, especially as it would have looked as if she was chasing after him a couple of days after meeting him.

So, here she was, at least an hour early for her shift and waiting for him to appear so she could find out whether he'd been given the news. Deep inside she felt a quiver of excitement that she would be in at the start of something momentous, but until he said something to let her know that the decision had been made public, she was just going to have to bite her tongue.

The sound of hurried footsteps coming along the corridor towards the staffroom had her looking up eagerly, but then the door slammed back against the rack of pigeonholes behind it, narrowly missing her on the way, and she saw Reg Smythe framed in the doorway with a face like thunder.

For several seconds he stood and glared at her, looking as if he was about to explode, then, rather than speaking, he brushed angrily past her and snatched the bundle of post waiting in his slot.

One letter in particular took his attention and he ripped the envelope open with hands that were almost trembling with suppressed emotion.

'It's bloody nonsense, that's what it is,' he snarled, clearly unconcerned who heard him as he scanned the contents. 'Wasting money, wasting resources…'

'Lily! Have you heard?' demanded Razak, suddenly appearing in front of her with a face wreathed in smiles. She'd been so focused on Reg's display of bad temper that she hadn't even realised that her immediate superior had entered the room.

'Heard what?' she asked automatically, as her heart gave a stupid leap in response to the man's sheer vitality. His dark eyes were almost glittering with suppressed emotion.

'As if you didn't know,' Reg sneered, as he crumpled the sheet of paper in one hand and flung it towards the bin. He didn't even react to the fact that it didn't make the distance, neither did he make any attempt to retrieve it. 'No wonder you were in such a hurry to avoid a conversation with me last night. An appointment to sort out your paperwork? Ha! Scurrying off to toady up to your new boss is more like it. Well, you might live to regret that decision, my girl. You'll find you've made the wrong choice when it gets to the end of his contract and no one wants you in their firm.' And with that warning still bouncing off the walls around her, he stomped out of the room.

'What on earth was that about?' Razak demanded of the room at large.

'Reg clearly isn't a happy bunny,' Colin offered wryly as he unfolded himself from a chair in the corner of the room. 'So that must mean that the decision's been made about your trial and you've got your way, but what it's all got to do with your new colleague I have no idea. She hasn't been here long enough to have any influence on the bean-counters.

'Anyway,' he continued, as he ambled across to retrieve his own post, 'congratulations, if you *have* got the go-ahead, and the best of luck to you. I can't say I'd ever want to work that way—too long in the tooth now to want to change my ways and hopefully too close to retirement for even the most eager bean-counter to try to force me to—but I'll be interested to see how it goes.'

'You've heard?' Lily asked, needing to hear the decision

in words of one syllable, although the question was totally redundant if Razak's delighted expression was anything to go by. 'Your trial has finally been approved?'

'The committee chairman was waiting for me as I came in this morning,' he said, surrounding her in an almost electric field of energy. 'Apparently, it had been pointed out to him that the theatre suite was almost finished and we would need some lead-in time to get everything organised for the first surgeries. So…' He took her arm in a gentle hold that belied the strength she knew he could use when needed, and led her to the opposite side of the room where there was some semblance of privacy.

Lily worried for a moment that he'd somehow found out that she had been the first one to have received the heavy hint that the decision had been made in his favour, afraid that he was about to demand why she hadn't found some way to let him know.

'I need to know if you're likely to change your mind,' he demanded bluntly, his gaze direct and uncompromising. 'You must have given it some thought since I explained what was going on. You already know that it'll mean long hours in a high-pressure experimental situation, but after *that*…' He gestured towards the door that had closed in Reg's wake. 'If you decide that it might be too much of a threat to your career to be associated with something so unpopular with the head of department…that it isn't right for you…'

'What on earth gave you the idea that I would be so indecisive?' she challenged, quite shocked that he would think it of her. 'I've had to fight every step of the way to get this far and unless you think I'm not up to the job, wild horses wouldn't drag me away. This is the sort of experiment that could actually do wonders for my career, to say nothing of the numbers of patients it could benefit.'

'There is also the sheer volume of experience you would amass in a relatively short period of time,' he pointed out, and she suddenly realised that this might be one of the reasons why *he* was so keen for the new regime to succeed. If he was leaving in a matter of months, it could be that he already had a more senior post lined up. In that case, the prospect of heading up such an innovative speciality within a specialty would stand him in equally good stead.

'So, have we got a firm date so we can get everything organised?' she demanded eagerly. 'How much longer are we going to have to wait before the suite will be signed off as fully equipped and ready?'

'I have a meeting at—' He got no further as his pager shrilled sharply. 'A and E,' he muttered, after retrieving it from his waist. He reached for the phone and Lily found herself holding her breath as she tried to hear what the voice on the other end of the line was saying.

Whatever it was, it must have been something horrific if the expression on Razak's face was anything to go by.

'Get on to the theatre manager and find out how soon there will be a table free,' he demanded, as soon as he put the phone down. She had to stride out to keep up with him as he set off at his usual cracking pace, his brain obviously working at the speed of light if the list of orders was anything to go by. She just hoped that she would be able to read her writing when the time came to decipher her hurried notes.

She had no idea yet how the incoming patient had amassed his injuries but already the paramedics had warned them that he had impacted fractures of both ankles, possible damage to his knees, hips and spine and severe trauma to his neck.

'We'll need ultrasound to check the circulation into his extremities. I'll let you know as soon as I can whether we'll need microsurgery for tendons and blood vessels. Can you check how long it will be if we need a CT scan and/or an MRI? I've no idea whether Plastics will need to be involved. I'll let you know when I see him.' The last words emerged just as the door swung shut behind him as he set off at full tilt down the stairs, obviously not wanting to risk a wait for a lift.

The next half an hour would have been a nightmare if the hospital hadn't recently seen sense and lifted its out-of-date ban on mobile phones. As it was, when the patient, Simon Bullen, left A and E, it was to go straight to the head of the queue for a CT scan, and by the time he was wheeled into Theatre the results of that and the full array of X-rays were on display.

Also ready and waiting was a full team of theatre personnel, half of whom had only just finished a busy night on call, and the fact that every one of them had seemed only too eager to work with Razak spoke volumes about the respect they had for him. In fact, the more she thought about it, the more she realised that, in spite of the relatively short time he'd been working there, he'd obviously impressed even some of those who'd been employed in the hospital for years.

The gleam in the women's eyes when they watched him stride into the room, his gloved hands held up and away from any chance of contamination, could be taken for another sort of eagerness. But that certainly wasn't the case with the anaesthetist, who'd willingly stayed on in spite of having only just finished a shift. Tim, it seemed, was one of Razak's more ardent supporters in his attempts to reorganise their operating methods.

'Ready when you are,' Tim called from his station. 'He's stable for the moment, but I'd be grateful if you could get in there and stop some of that blood loss pretty soon or, as fast as I'm pushing the fluids in, he'll go into hypovolaemic shock.'

'What on earth did he do to himself?' Lily demanded in shock when she got her first good look at the pictures lined up along the view boxes. 'Tib and fib in both ankles, both femurs, three lumbar vertebrae with compression fractures, two cervical vertebrae with avulsion fractures and his right humerus shattered just above the elbow joint.'

'The paramedics said it's a failed attempt at hanging himself,' Tim said over the sounds of the various items of monitoring equipment that surrounded him, obviously following everything going on in the theatre even though his eyes were focussed on his dials. 'Apparently, he climbed up into his roof and tied a rope to the rafters then climbed down and jumped off the top of the stairs.'

'And?' prompted one of the nurses in tones of horrified fascination.

'And the rope broke,' Tim finished almost ghoulishly, prompting a round of groans and half-hidden winces.

'That explains everything except the broken humerus,' said the scrub nurse from the other side of the table.

'Hit the banister on the way down?' Lily suggested, the picture only too clear in her mind. With the man landing feet first from such a height, it was small wonder that his ankles, femurs and lumbar vertebrae had been fractured. It was a common set of injuries when parachutes failed to open. The gruesome part, to her way of thinking, were the avulsion fractures caused before the rope had broken. The man had literally broken his neck and survived—so far.

'Where are we going to start?' she asked Razak, as she compiled a tentative list in her own head.

'Well, his neck's going to need Colin's skills to stabilise it, and he'll be in Theatre with his own patient for at least another hour. Luckily, that's relatively stable with the collar on. The CT scan of his head is good and there were no apparent visceral injuries on the ultrasound. So, at the moment, the most pressing thing is the blood loss into that thigh, so let's get moving, please.'

They all knew, without Razak having to say any more, that the blood loss into the surrounding tissues after such a break could be life-threatening.

'Peripheral pulses have gone,' warned Tim, as Razak began his initial incision, letting them know that their patient must have already lost approximately thirty per cent of his total blood volume. There was very little blood loss evident on the outside of his body so that left the scenario of profuse bleeding somewhere inside and Lily was glad that she'd ordered plenty of replacement fluids.

They definitely couldn't wait for the arrival of the specifically cross-matched supplies—as it was, it looked as if they were going to use all of the O negative before it came. In the meantime, she was hard-pressed to keep up with Razak's lightning-fast decisions once the shattered femur was exposed, more impressed than ever by the way he could seem so cool and calm in such a high-risk situation.

CHAPTER FOUR

RAZAK had long ago learned what was meant when someone was said to 'raise their game' but he'd never seen such a prime example until today.

If he hadn't seen a copy of Lily's CV detailing her relative inexperience as a surgeon, he would never have guessed it. At every stage of their complicated task, from finding and isolating a shredded vein in the man's thigh and clamping it, ready for the vascular surgeon to repair, to taking over the management of one of the ankle fractures entirely, she was very impressive.

Both legs had suffered fractures of the tibia and fibula and would require screwing and pinning of the medial malleolus and plating of the tibia to restore mobility and reduce the severity of traumatic arthritis, but with the patient already stressed by the length of time he'd been on the table, Razak been wondering just how he was going to manage to effect the repairs in a reasonable length of time.

'Do you want me to begin on his other ankle?' Lily had suggested quietly, as soon as the surgical site on the thigh had been satisfactorily closed. Colin had been and gone, leaving the patient's head and neck enclosed in the cage of metal that would prevent any movement in his spine while his fractured vertebrae healed, and the vascular surgeon had gone to join one of the Plastics team who had the unenviable job of trying to piece together an arm that had gone through a plate-glass window.

Razak looked up from the complicated jigsaw of broken bones that he was trying to piece together and was almost taken aback by the calm confidence in those cool grey-blue eyes.

He dragged his eyes away for another analytical look at the X-rays of the other limb before meeting her gaze again.

'Have you done a Steinmann pin unassisted before?' he challenged, and saw one slender eyebrow lift briefly.

'Once,' she admitted honestly. 'Closely supervised.'

'Well, they do joke that learning surgery is a matter of see one, do one, teach one, don't they?' he said wryly. Then he gave a nod of permission. 'But tell me if you start to have any problems.'

'Of course,' she said quietly, but he'd heard the edge of excitement in her voice that told him she was eager for the new challenge.

In the event, she had no problems at all, her handiwork meticulous as she positioned the broken segment of the fibula and held it with just the right number of screws through the slim plate she'd angled to fit precisely. The screw and Steinmann pin needed to relocate the segment that had been broken off the tibia were a little more complicated, but only because both of them were trying to work in the same limited space.

Even so, her concentration on the job in hand seemed to be much better than his own, his thoughts jolted by every inadvertent brush of her willowy body against his, her slender arm or the curve of her hip. It was both a relief and a disappointment when he finished his work on the man's ankle and moved away from her to work on the damaged elbow. Then, with all the procedures completed, she straightened up and met his gaze and he realised that the distraction might not have been one-sided.

She tried to hide it, tearing her eyes away from his and quickly hurrying into speech, but when he saw the soft bloom of colour spreading up her throat from the loose V of the faded green scrub top and into her cheeks and registered the tell-tale urgency of her pulse in the side of her slender throat, he knew.

'Good work,' Tim pronounced in satisfied tones, and snapped Razak out of his crazy preoccupation.

What on earth was he thinking? No matter how beautiful or how alluring she was, the woman was a junior colleague. He would be leaving himself open to all sorts of accusations if he were to make any advances. He certainly didn't want to go back to his own country with a suit for sexual harassment hanging over him.

'How are his vital signs?' he demanded, hoping no one else could hear the revealing roughness in his voice. Gossip was something else he could do without.

'He's a hell of a lot more stable than he was when he got here,' Tim said wryly. 'In fact, now that you've got all the hardware installed, he's almost perfect...until he tries it again.'

That was enough to sober them all up from the heady feeling at the end of successful surgery.

'Do you really think he'll try to hang himself again?' Lily gasped, clearly horrified by the idea.

Tim gave a slightly hollow laugh. 'I doubt he'd try the same method again—at least, not with the same rope.'

'Tim! That's enough!' warned one of the more senior theatre nurses. 'You really are a gruesome man.'

'Unfortunately, he may be right,' Razak said, resigned to the foibles of his fellow man. 'It doesn't matter how long we take to put him back together, if he's determined to end his life, sooner or later he will succeed.'

For a moment it looked as if Lily was going to add something to the conversation but, unaware that he was watching her, she shook her head and briefly rested one gloved hand on the man's shoulder in a gesture that almost looked like a benediction.

Even as he watched her strip her gloves off and lob the neat package into the bin he could see that she was preoccupied and somehow knew that, at some stage, she would make a point of going up to the ward to visit the man. It was unlikely that her effort would make any difference to the eventual outcome, but...but it was exactly what he'd intended doing, too.

He felt a strange shiver travel the length of his spine at the thought that they might have more than their love of surgery in common. So many of his colleagues seemed quite content to do an operation to the best of their ability while keeping a clinical distance between themselves and the person on the table. Did he and Lily share the same very different attitude?

Then he realised just how far his thoughts had strayed from the job in hand and he deliberately wiped away all such extraneous thoughts. He had a critically ill patient to check up on, and wasting his time on frivolous thoughts of his far-too-beautiful colleague definitely wasn't on his agenda.

Except, that night, he realised it wasn't going to be quite that easy to banish those images from his brain.

It wasn't just the fact that the two of them seemed to work in perfect synchronicity in Theatre. He'd seen it happen before but only with surgeons who had become accustomed to each other's ways through many hours of working together. With Lily…it was almost as though their brains were tuned to the same frequency so that he barely needed to speak for her to know what he needed from her.

It was an exhilarating sensation, so that he'd felt almost as if he had been flying, but it was dangerous, too. Neither of them could afford to become involved with each other in any way other than professionally, but it certainly hadn't felt like a professional connection between the two of them when he'd met her eyes over the unflattering edge of her mask. He'd actually found himself noticing that, far from being a flat grey-blue colour, there was a green-gold circle around her pupils that radiated out like rays of light across the silvery iris all the way towards the dark sapphire-blue rim.

'What on earth…?' he exclaimed, wondering what had come over him. He couldn't recall ever having paid so much attention to the colour of a woman's eyes before. 'And I shouldn't be now!' he said fiercely, as he reached for the phone. He would phone Karim. A conversation with his irreverent half-brother would be guaranteed to take his mind off Dr Lily Langley.

'So, what's your new boss like, then, Lil?' Rose asked in the tone that told Lily that she was settling down for a gossip.

Unfortunately, when she'd phoned, it had been in the hope that a conversation with her mother would take her mind off Razak Khan. She should have known that it wouldn't work, not with her mother's insatiable curiosity.

'I bet he's middle-aged and married,' she heard Iris call from somewhere in the background. 'With all his muscles gone to flab once he got too old to play rugby.'

Suddenly Lily knew that it would be disastrous if she gave her family even a *hint* of how good-looking Razak was. Her sisters already taunted her with the fact that she hadn't managed to 'hook herself a doctor' yet. If they found out that her new boss had sparked hormones to life that she hadn't even known existed, she would never hear the end of it.

'He's foreign and temporary,' she said, hoping she sounded suitably dismissive. 'He'll be going back to his own country in a few months.'

She had to wait while her mother relayed the information to whoever else was in the room with her and, as she'd expected, Iris was ready with a pointed comment.

'Bad luck, Lil. Still, his replacement might be worth looking at,' she suggested, raising her voice so that her mother didn't need to relay her comments. 'Hey, I heard that those orthopaedic surgeons are making an absolute fortune doing private operations, and that's on top of their ordinary salary. Is it true? You could retire straight away if you hooked one of them.'

'At the moment I'm too busy to do anything about hooking anyone,' Lily said crossly. 'I barely know my way around the hospital yet, and there have been accident victims needing operations as well as those booked in for replacement joints and so on.'

'Ooh, I really don't know how you could do all that gory stuff,' her mother said with an audible shudder. 'Honestly, I don't know where you got the idea from…to go and be a surgeon. You could have been a GP. Then you could have come and worked at the practice in town here, and moved back home again. There'd be no shortage of people to choose from. You know most of the boys because you went to school with them…or your sisters did. Marjorie's son has just moved back again since his wife went off with that estate agent and Derek's just set up his own plumbing business. They're both good lads and I'm sure you could take your pick of—'

'Mum, I haven't finished my training yet, so I'm really not interested,' she interrupted hastily. 'I've got at least another year before I can—'

'Another year! But, Lily, love, you're already thirty!' her mother exclaimed, as if Lily didn't know her own age. 'You can't afford to wait any longer to start a family. They said on the telly just the other night that too many women are waiting until they've got a career and then when they try for a baby, they find it's too late…that their eggs have all shrivelled up or something. You *can't* wait any longer if you're going to have a lovely family like Iris and—'

'Mum, there was a woman the other year who had her first baby when she was in her sixties.'

'What? No! That's awful!' Rose exclaimed, momentarily diverted from her usual plaint. 'The poor little mite! Imagine having a mother old enough to be your great-grandmother! *You're* not thinking of doing that, are you?'

'Of course not, Mum. I only mentioned it to show that I've got a few years yet before I need to panic and leap into bed with the first reasonably healthy man who offers.'

Lily managed to sustain the rest of the conversation with only half of her attention, her mother exclaiming at length over the idea of 'geriatric' mothers.

At least it had switched her attention from her unmarried daughter's shortcomings, but it couldn't take Lily's own thoughts away from Razak Khan.

She could just imagine what Iris would have said if she'd found out that not only was her new boss close to her own age but he was seriously good-looking. As for single…

'I have absolutely no idea,' she said aloud into the echoing solitude of her minute bathroom a little later, suddenly aware that her stomach had taken a dive towards her feet at the thought that Razak might, at this very moment, be curled up in bed, making love with his stunningly beautiful, endlessly fascinating wife.

'Not that it makes a scrap of difference to me whether he's married or not,' she said firmly through a mouthful of toothpaste, even as she realised that she was lying through her freshly brushed teeth.

So what if he was the first man whose mouth had made her wonder what his kiss would taste like, whose eyes spoke to her of knowledge far beyond her wildest imagining and whose body fascinated her every time she came within its aura of leashed power so that he had even started invading her dreams. She, Lily Langley, who had never dreamed of anything beyond achieving her goal of a consultancy and leading her own team…

What she really needed was someone to talk to, but there was no one.

'I certainly can't talk to anyone in the family,' she declared with a shudder. She could just imagine the uproar *that* would cause. First there would be amazement at the mere suggestion that she was attracted to a man. Then, if she was stupid enough to let slip that the man was her boss…well, it didn't bear thinking about.

Her father would recognise that the situation could end up as professional suicide but her mother would be going all misty-eyed over wedding dresses and the next brood of grandchildren while her sisters would be crowing and twittering that Lily had finally hooked herself a consultant.

As if anyone as insignificant as Lily could ever hook someone like Razak when, by all accounts, every single nurse in the hospital had set her cap at him, and a few of the married ones, too, if the gossips were right.

'Why now?' she groaned aloud into the darkness as sleep *still* eluded her. For years her imagination had been limited to devising ways of piecing shattered bones together. Why had it suddenly taken off in an entirely new direction so that when he'd pulled his mask down at the end of the operation and grinned at her at their success, it had started devising ways for that sexy mouth to meet hers and teach her all the ways to please him?

She finally fell asleep to X-rated dreams, waking up with a burning need to see the man, if only to prove to herself that it had been mere exhaustion that had made him seem so overwhelmingly attractive.

Please, *please*, let there be no hitches in getting the new theatre suites up and running, she pleaded fervently as she made her way up to the surgical ward before the start of her shift.

After her feverish hurry to get to the hospital, she was suddenly loath to come face to face with the man who was dominating her thoughts, afraid that he might be able to see that she was aware of him with every cell in her body. It was safer by far to detour for a quick visit to each of their post-operative patients just to satisfy herself that there hadn't been any problems overnight.

'You're bright and early this morning, Dr Langley,' said the staff nurse as she entered the female half of the ward. She was looking a little frazzled, as though it had been an especially busy night. 'Is there something I should know about? Mr Khan just phoned to warn me he was on his way up.'

Just the sound of his name was enough to double Lily's pulse rate and she would have turned tail and run if it wouldn't have caused just the sort of gossip she didn't want.

'Please, won't you call me Lily when there aren't any patients about?' she suggested, giving herself a moment to get her brain working before she had to say anything intelligent. She'd thought she'd been giving herself a few extra minutes to get her crazy emotions under control by coming onto the ward, but Razak was already on his way. Any moment now, he would walk through that door and that sexy voice would say…

'Good morning, Lily.'

She closed her eyes and concentrated on breathing…in and out, in and out. How could he sound even sexier with every time she heard him speak? And as for looking at him… She opened her eyes again and found the staff nurse watching her with a knowing look in her eyes.

For a second panic struck her like a wrecking ball and she was terrified that the young woman would say something that would give her away. Her fear must have shown on her face because there was an answering half-smile of understanding. Then all it took was the slightest of shake of Jo's head to indicate that she wouldn't spill the beans, which allowed Lily's panic to ease.

'Good morning, Mr Khan,' she said with a modicum of her composure restored. 'I came up to have a look at the patients we operated on yesterday. Did you need me for something else?'

'For now, let us pay a visit to our patients,' he said with a smile, but not before she caught a glimpse of something else in those dark, dark eyes. A glint of…what? Something she hadn't ever seen in a man's eyes before, certainly not when he was looking in *her* direction.

'Would you like to start with Mrs Turner?' Jo suggested easily. 'She's been reminding me every time I've gone past her that she wants to have a word with you as soon as possible.'

'There is a problem?' Razak demanded, his expression all business in an instant. 'Her pain is bad? She needs more analgesia?'

'Not at all!' Jo laughed as she cheerfully handed him the file she'd been checking and updating ready for handover. 'The opposite, if anything. Go and see.'

Lily was glad of her long legs as he strode swiftly along to Mrs Turner's room. As it was, she was hard-pushed to keep up with him until he came to a halt beside the elderly woman's bedside.

'Mrs Turner, I understand that you wanted to speak to me. Is there some problem I can help you—?'

'Oh, not at all!' Cicely Turner interrupted with a broad smile. 'I just couldn't wait to thank you…to thank you both. I just can't believe that all that dreadful gnawing pain has gone. Completely gone, as if you'd waved a magic wand!'

'Well, I'm glad about that, Mrs—'

'I tell you, I was expecting to wake up in agony after such a big operation,' their patient interrupted, clearly bubbling over with enthusiasm. 'Especially when you told me what you were going to have to do to me when you got me on the table…dislocate my hip, chop part of it off, hammer a new bit in… It all sounded like the sort of thing my husband used to do in his workshop at the end of the garden.'

'So…' Razak tried again when she paused for breath but still couldn't stop her.

'Well, of course, I'm a bit sore where you had to cut me, but the stuff the nurse gave me took that away. But it's all thanks to the two of you that I can actually lie down and sit up and even stand up without a single twinge of that dreadful unrelenting bone-deep agony. I've been living with pain for more than two years, you know,' she said, and pressed her lips into a tight line at the memory. 'It was nearly six months before I gave in and asked my GP to get me an appointment with a specialist, then, after waiting months and months to see him, I was told I was going to have to wait up to a year before he would be able to do my operation. If the hospital hadn't taken you two on, I'd probably still be waiting.'

Lily met Jo's eyes on the other side of the bed and saw that she'd known exactly what was going to happen when the two of them visited her patient. She saw, too, the moment she decided to take pity on them.

'So, Cicely, would you like to slide down in the bed a bit so we can show the sawbones how you're doing?'

'Oh, of course, dear,' she agreed readily, before turning back to Razak and Lily even as she complied. 'She's been taking ever such good care of me,' she confided. 'And she makes a lovely cup of tea. Just right. Not too milky but not too strong either.'

While the anti-embolic stocking was rolled down to allow them to check on the colour and texture of Cicely's skin, both Lily and Razak took advantage of the time to pull on sterile gloves, each taking the extra precaution of using the bacteriostatic gel before they went anywhere near the wound along the side of the patient's upper thigh. The last thing their patient needed was to have an infective agent introduced at this stage by sloppy hygiene procedures.

'Nice neat stitches,' Razak commented as they were revealed, and his approval spread a warm glow through Lily. 'The wound drains are doing their job well and there are no signs of any redness or untoward discharge. In fact, everything looks exactly the way it should,' he pronounced as he straightened up.

'Well, you did promise me that you would do your best, and you've certainly kept your promise,' their patient said with a beam as Jo rolled on a clean anti-embolic stocking and pulled the cotton gown back into position. 'Now it's all up to me to get back on my feet. I'll be going to stay with one of my children when I'm discharged from hospital, but I have every intention of being back in my own home before summer comes. It will soon be time to start sowing bedding plants for my garden and all my neighbours depend on me to do a few trays for them, too.'

'You won't be tempted to do too much, too soon, will you?' Lily cautioned gently, even as she applauded the woman's zest for life.

'I certainly won't be doing anything that will mess up your good work,' she promised. 'I've already been memorising the list of instructions you gave me. No crossing my legs…so I'll be putting a small pillow between my knees so I can't forget; no flexing the hip more than forty-five degrees… so one of my sons is getting me a wedge-shaped cushion to put in my chair; no rotational movement…so I've cancelled my dancing lessons…and I was really looking forward to learning to do the twist!'

'I'm glad you're feeling so cheerful,' Razak said through their shared laughter, and patted her blue-veined hand. 'You look after yourself.' And he led the way out of the room.

'You might want to see Gary Freshett next,' Jo suggested, when she joined them again to hand Razak the next set of case notes.

'Any particular reason?' he queried.

'Only that he hasn't got any—reason, that is,' Jo said quietly. 'He's only hours post-operative and I've already caught him getting out of bed twice, trying to see how far he can bend his knee.'

Lily remembered the man all too clearly. He was heading ungraciously towards middle age while still trying to pretend that he could do everything that he could do as a young aspiring sportsman. But it had been his unpleasant leer at her while she'd been trying to make sure that he'd understood what his operation involved that had struck her most forcefully.

The fact that he was now ignoring everything he'd been told was probably par for the course with a man of his arrogance.

'Good morning, Mr Freshett. I hear you've been trying to mess all our good work up,' Razak said crisply as he approached the man's bed, and Lily silently cheered that her boss wasn't going to pull his punches.

'Well, I don't want to waste any time lying around in

hospital when I could be getting back on the golf course,' he snapped impatiently. 'I've got a good chance of getting my name on the club trophy this year so I need to get my knee moving again.'

'And how many weeks is it until the competition is played, or is it a cumulative one?' Razak queried mildly, as though he was genuinely interested in the game when Lily already knew, on his own admission, that he'd rather watch paint dry.

'Cumulative, so I can't afford to miss more than a couple of matches or I won't stand a chance of catching up. That's why it's so important to get this damn knee moving as soon as possible, otherwise—'

'Mr Freshett,' Razak interrupted sharply. 'Didn't you listen to *anything* that Dr Langley told you yesterday? She went through the whole operation with you and told you exactly how many weeks of physiotherapy and rehabilitation it would take before you could even *start* to play golf again.'

'Well, yes...but that's only for the wimps who can't take a bit of discomfort and don't care about winning,' he said dismissively. 'I've been a sportsman all my life and I know how far I can push myself.'

'And *I* know what it will do to your knee if you *do* push yourself,' Razak snapped. 'There is a *reason* why you were given that timetable, a sound *medical* reason. So let me give you another item to put on that timetable. If you try to go on the golf course before you have completed your post-operative period, you will end up on my operating table before the last game of the season has even been played, and this time I won't be removing the osteophytes that were hampering your movement. I will be operating to fuse your knee so that it will never bend again because you will have ruined the joint permanently. Unless you follow your instructions to the letter, I doubt that you will *ever* get your name on that trophy.'

There was an uncomfortably chastened silence in the room as he continued with his examination of their handiwork, and he pronounced himself satisfied with progress with the minimum of facial expression before he stalked out of the room.

Lily followed him in silence until they were well out of earshot before she queried in an innocent voice, 'So what exactly would prevent Gary Freshett from being a candidate for a knee joint replacement if he messes the osteotomy up?'

'If he messes it up by deliberately doing too much weight-bearing and flexion too soon, he will have proved that he is too stupid and arrogant to be given a joint replacement,' Razak snapped.

Lily deliberately stayed silent for several seconds before she raised her eyes to meet his, but she couldn't prevent the corners of her mouth quivering as she fought a grin.

'Too stupid for a joint replacement?' she said softly.

'Don't forget arrogant,' he reminded her, then flung both hands up in the air. 'Damn it all, it was his crazy need to prove he's some super-stud sportsman that caused the damage in the first place. We worked hard to give him as much range of movement as we could and to make him as pain-free as possible, and he's trying to ruin it all before the anaesthetic is fully out of his body.'

'His life, his body, his choice,' Lily chanted softly. 'That's what one of our tutors told us in the early days of our training. He said that all we could do was our best. The rest was up to the patient.'

'And on that note it's time to go and see how Mr Bullen is doing,' Razak said with a slightly unsettling air of resignation.

'Apparently, he's off ventilation,' Lily offered. 'He's still in ICU on diminishing levels of monitoring, but will be moved out if they get a more acute patient needing the space.'

When they reported their arrival to the senior sister on ICU, just the mention of Simon Bullen was enough to garner a reaction.

'Is there a problem, Sister?' Razak asked, with a worried glance in Lily's direction. They both knew just how long it had taken to repair Simon's injuries and how complex the surgery had been. Had they managed to miss something vital?

'Only the fact that he doesn't want to be here,' she said cryptically.

'In ICU?' Lily asked.

'Alive,' Maura Philips corrected grimly. 'He's only been conscious a short while but he's been making my staff's lives such a misery that almost any one of them would willingly do the job for him just to shut him up.'

'So he's not going to be showering us with gratitude for putting the jigsaw back together again, then?'

'No. We've actually had to move him into the isolation bay at the far end of the unit because he was upsetting the other patients and visitors.'

'Well, then, perhaps it's time to find out if he's got any genuine grievances,' Razak suggested grimly, and gestured for Sister Philips to lead the way.

CHAPTER FIVE

INITIALLY, Lily was happy to stay in the background—after all, Razak was the consultant and hadn't really needed to have her with him.

She couldn't fault the way he greeted the man surrounded by all the high-tech monitoring equipment, his manner as polite and courteous as ever. She was concerned when the man merely glared at them when Razak enquired about the level of pain he was suffering, but this turned to anger when the man finally opened his mouth.

'Interfering bloody busybodies!' he railed in a voice that sounded painfully raw as he forced it out through the bruised tissues of his throat. He spat out a string of foul curses. 'Why couldn't you just let me die? I *wanted* to die. I've got nothing left to live for. Nothing! She's taken it all away.'

'Mr Bullen,' Razak began gently, 'we were only doing our job and—'

'Only doing your job?' he interrupted rudely, and laughed hoarsely, but there was no humour in the sound. 'That's what the lawyer said, the divorce lawyer who helped her to take everything from me…my house, my business… I don't care about them. I could always start again…set up a new business, buy another house…but she's told so many lies, alienated all my friends and even took my dog…' He tried to wipe away the tell-tale tears but the arm he chose was the one they'd had to repair after its shattering contact with the banister rail. He angrily brushed away Lily's silent offer of a handful of tissues.

'Anyway, why would you care how I am?' the man challenged with a rapid return to belligerence. 'Look at you with your expensive suit, silk tie and hand-made shoes. What would you know about the lives of ordinary people? You just patch them up and forget about them once they hobble out of the door.'

Lily had reached the end of her patience.

'Mr Bullen,' she said sharply. 'I want you to take a look at these.' Anger at his unwarranted attack on Razak had put a fine tremor in her hands but she still managed to slot the set of X-rays onto the view box with icy precision.

'These are your X-rays. They show your ankles—Mr Khan and I actually operated on one each, putting in plates and screws to rebuild the bones so you would be able to walk again. This picture shows the pin we had to put in to repair your thigh. You were bleeding so much from this injury that by the time we got you on the table you'd already lost nearly a third of your blood volume and you were in danger of kidney failure. This one is of your lower back and those bits there are the vertebrae with the crush fractures that we can do nothing about except to wait for them to heal and stabilise. You will probably always suffer from backache as a result.'

She had to pause a second to draw breath but she didn't dare to glance at Razak. Was he furious that she'd intervened when she was nothing more than his junior?

'This,' she continued, as she slapped up the next plate, 'is your elbow. You were extremely lucky that the break didn't involve the joint itself. As it is, once that's mended it probably won't give you any problems other than aching when the weather changes. But *this* one…' She tapped the monochromatic evidence of the damage done to the man's neck by his inexpertly tied knot. 'This is the prize exhibit. *This* one is the reason why you've got the Meccano set attached to your head because *this* is where you broke your neck.'

'Broke my—'

She was on a roll now, and he had no chance of interrupting.

'You could have died instantly…which is obviously what you were intending…or you could just have paralysed yourself, but instead you had a whole team of people—many of whom had already worked their full shift that day but we all stayed on, just for you—who worked damn hard on you for hours to put you back together. And all you can do is curse at us for interfering?'

He was definitely a little stunned by her unexpected vehemence and for a moment he even had the grace to look shamefaced but then his expression closed up.

'You shouldn't have bothered,' he said quietly, at least this time without the profanities. 'There's no point. I've got nothing and no one—not even a dog any more.'

'That's not true,' she argued, as she approached the side of the bed. 'You've got *you*.' She reached out a hand to touch his wrist, wondering if she was completely wasting her time. 'You're a good-looking man and you're probably quite intelligent if you've managed to set up a successful business.

You speak well, even if your vocabulary is a bit repetitive at times, and if you like animals you can always adopt a rescued one…they need your love even more than one that's never known cruelty. I'd say you've got plenty of bait to go fishing and there are definitely plenty more fish in the sea…'

She finally wound down with an uncomfortable feeling that she'd said far more than she should have, but it would all have been worth it if even one of the things she'd said penetrated the man's depression.

She felt her cheeks heat up when she realised that she'd used her own sister's analogy of hooking a mate, and with Razak listening in, too.

The lengthening silence was broken by the irritating bleep of someone's pager and when Razak stepped outside the room to answer the call, their patient's eyes followed him thoughtfully out of the door.

'The two of you work together a lot?' he asked.

'Hours at a time,' she said, and was so cheered by this first indication that he was thinking about something other than his own situation that it loosened the strings on her tongue. 'So you can tell I definitely know what I'm talking about when I speak about good-looking men.'

Simon Bullen's eyes flicked away to something over her shoulder and with a dreadful sense of inevitability she turned to see that Razak had come back into the room. For several endless seconds he held her gaze with his and she wished the highly polished floor would open up and swallow her.

'Thank you for that kind testimonial, Dr Langley,' he said without a flicker of reaction, 'but that was Tim telling us that our first patient is ready for Theatre.'

* * *

So she thought he was good-looking, Razak mused as he strode swiftly ahead of her, hoping she couldn't see the grin spreading across his face.

It was one thing to find her attractive but it was another thing entirely to discover that she felt the same way. So good for the ego.

Not that he hadn't had any number of women attracted to him before, but there could be so many reasons for that...his family's wealth being the primary draw for some women and his slightly exotic looks for others.

Which was it for Lily? She'd commented on his looks when she hadn't realised he'd been able to overhear her but...was he a fool for hoping that she would be one of the few who saw him as a doctor first and foremost, that she would see beyond the surface trappings?

Not that he could act on it even if she did, no matter what the woman did to his blood pressure.

He gave a silent huff of laughter when he remembered the way she'd read the Riot Act to Simon Bullen. She certainly had fire in her belly and didn't care who knew it. And he'd thought she would be one of those stereotypical repressed English women, cool to the point of frigidity and totally unable to let their hair down, even in the bedroom.

'Bad move,' he growled softly, when the thoughts of Lily and bedroom collided in his head. It would have to be enough for him that he'd realised she was so much more than he'd anticipated and that he already knew that she was going to be a key player in the eventual success of the new unit.

'Anything else is strictly off limits,' he said aloud, as the door to the changing room swung shut behind him and he began to strip his suit off…as if *that* would stop his imagination.

Things didn't get any better when he strode into Theatre ten minutes later to be greeted by the sexy wail of a saxophone.

'Who chose the music?' he asked in surprise. Tim usually opted for something with a driving rock beat while his choice veered between classical instrumental works or his latest introduction, evocative unaccompanied voices singing traditional Gaelic songs.

'I did,' said Lily behind him, and he pivoted to face her, strangely delighted to find that she'd surprised him again. 'Tim said it was my turn to choose today, and then he pulled a face when it came on.'

'So you like blues.'

'And jazz,' she elaborated. 'But preferably instrumental when I'm trying to concentrate.'

'Well, let's see if it works,' he suggested, as he waved her towards the table to which their first patient had just been transferred.

He waited until she was just inches away from him before he drew in the familiar perfume that followed her wherever she went.

'So,' he murmured under the cover of the sounds of the empty trolley leaving the theatre and the swing doors thumping shut. 'You listen to jazz and you wear jasmine.' Her wide eyes flicked up to him with an almost startled expression in them and when he refused to let her look away, he actually saw the moment when awareness replaced her surprise.

Silently, he was berating himself for instigating even this tiny bit of intimacy between them but it had been irresistible…

She was irresistible, with more facets than a brilliant-cut diamond.

Enough! Concentrate!

He drew in a deep breath and blew it out through his mouth in a steady stream into his mask, where no one else would see what he was doing to bring his thoughts back under control.

'Our patient is Chloe Westerham,' he announced to the room at large. 'She's seventeen years old and has been undergoing chemo for a tumour in her tibia. The tumour has greatly reduced in size but to make sure there's no recurrence or spread of the cancer there's no way we can remove it without taking a significant amount of the bone as well. That leaves us with two logical choices, amputation, which in a girl of this age would be devastating, especially as she's a keen sportswoman and dancer, or a titanium replacement.'

Lily let Razak's slightly husky accent flow around her while she tried to get her rioting emotions under control. She didn't need to concentrate on his words because the two of them had already discussed what he'd decided to do during Chloe's operation.

She had no doubts about her ability to assist him during the young woman's surgery. There was something about working with him that seemed to give her the confidence to feel that she could do almost anything.

What she didn't know was why her emotions were so scrambled. What was it about this man in particular that had her hormones in an uproar? It had never happened before so she couldn't understand why a single dark-eyed glance across the operating table… No, not even that. He just had to walk into the room and her heart beat faster.

It just wasn't logical. She'd spent so many years concentrating on achieving her goal without being even remotely sidetracked by her male colleagues, while *he*…

She ventured a look at him, his dark hair covered by a pale blue disposable cap that should have done nothing for his masculinity, and at least half of his face hidden behind the ubiquitous mask. She could see no more of him than she could of Tim, ensconced behind his dials and cylinders, but Tim had never made her heart skip so much as a single beat where Razak…

'Hey, Jazz, are you still with us?' his husky voice demanded, snapping her out of her introspection, and there was something fiercely intimate in the gaze that held hers.

Startled by the heat and almost afraid of her own reaction to it, she swiftly dragged her eyes away and back down to the job in hand.

Surely there hadn't been anything in what he could see of her expression that would have given her thoughts away. That would be just too embarrassing.

Thank goodness she could see exactly what it was that he needed her to do without having to ask. At least the rest of the team wouldn't have to know that her concentration had wavered.

'Is that Lily's new nickname?' Tim demanded with a spark of curiosity from the head of the table.

'Because she likes jazz,' confirmed the scrub nurse, sounding knowledgeable. After all, she'd been listening to their conversation about the choice of today's music when Razak had come into Theatre.

Lily flicked her eyes up to meet his, startled to find that they were waiting for her, and realised that only she knew that her taste in music was no more than half of the story.

There and then she decided that she was going to get rid of every one of her jasmine-scented toiletries and replace them with something completely different.

'Don't change it. It suits you,' he murmured softly, almost as if he'd been listening in on her private thoughts, and that unnerved her even more.

By the end of the surgery, the only conclusion she'd come to was that she needed a few minutes to think… some time to get her head in order before she had to concentrate on the next case. She was part of a team and each patient deserved her best, not a brain that was focussed more on the lead surgeon and her feelings towards him.

Desperately needing to avoid Razak while she did her soul-searching, she'd stayed in Theatre, checking and re-checking her part of the case notes to allow him to get well away. She barely stopped herself groaning aloud when the phone rang as she was about to leave and the receptionist on the other end asked to speak to Razak.

'Can I give him a message?' she offered. He was the last person she wanted to have to speak to. 'I'm Dr Langley, his junior, and we've just finished our first case, so he's probably in the staffroom, having something to drink. I could fetch him if you want to wait.'

'Oh.' There was a world of indecision in that single syllable. 'He's got a long-distance phone call from someone who says he's Mr Khan's brother.'

'Switch him through and I'll see if I can take a message. If not, I can suggest a time for him to try to ring back,' Lily said with a sudden surge of curiosity. Thoughts of her charismatic boss filled most of her waking and sleeping moments, but she really knew very little about him. The thought of speaking to his brother had a special appeal.

'Hello. This is Karim Khan. To whom am I speaking?' said a voice with a rather heavier version of Razak's attractive accent but without the husky note to his voice that made her every nerve quiver.

'I'm Lily Langley, a surgeon who works with your brother. Can I give him a message for you?'

'I really need to speak with him. Is there some way he could come to the phone?'

'It might take a few minutes but I'll go and find him straight away,' she offered, hearing strain and urgency in his voice and wondering at the situation that had put them there. 'If you get cut off in the meantime, I'll tell him to ring you straight back.'

'You are most kind. Thank you so much,' he said with a degree of courtesy that she thought had long since disappeared. But there was no time to ponder comparative standards of politeness.

Depositing the receiver on the desk, she hurried out into the corridor and was relieved that the first person she saw was Razak.

The second person was Reg and from the expression on his florid face this was not a friendly conversation.

The difference between the two men couldn't have been greater as they faced each other. As he was part of the way through an operating shift, Razak was in a set of the usual washed-to-death cotton scrubs with a pair of white clogs on his feet. By comparison, Mr Smythe in his expensive suit should have looked superior but it was Razak who was the embodiment of leashed power as he stood listening.

'Well, Khan, you might have *temporarily* got your own

way over using the new theatre suite but *I'm* the head of the orthopaedic department,' Reg was saying, obviously well into a carefully prepared speech. 'And *I'm* telling you that you can't expect to hog any more time in the other theatre rosters. The rest of the surgeons have patients to fit in… patients who have been waiting for the extra operating capacity to come on line, only to have *you* take it away.'

'Of course I realise that the timetables will have to be altered, Mr Smythe,' Razak began patiently, and Lily had no doubt that he would eventually have found some way to calm the man down but there wasn't time for a lengthy round of hospital politics.

'Excuse me,' she interrupted, her hurried strides taking her to their side in a matter of seconds. 'There's an urgent phone call for you, Mr Khan. I left the phone off the hook in the anteroom. The caller said his name was Karim and that he's your brother. He was most insistent—' She didn't get any further before Razak was making his hasty apologies to Mr Smythe.

'I am so sorry, sir, but my father has been unwell and if this is my brother calling then I *must* take the call. If we could speak later?' He barely paused long enough for Reg's grudging nod before he strode away, leaving Lily alone with their department head.

She could almost feel sorry for the man. He'd obviously pumped himself up for the confrontation and was now left without a legitimate target on which to vent his spleen… although the malevolent expression in his eyes told her that he'd very much like to let fly at her.

'Tell Khan that I'll be in the staffroom,' he snapped, and stomped off down the corridor.

Lily was left wondering which way to go. She hardly wanted to follow the department head into the staffroom. By now he was probably regaling anyone who would listen with his grievances. But she could hardly return towards the operating theatres either, or it would look as if she was intent on eavesdropping on Razak's conversation with his brother.

Even as she hovered indecisively, the senior administrator with whom she'd had her meeting came striding along the corridor towards her.

'Do you know where I can find Mr Khan?' he demanded, and the deep pleat between his eyebrows filled her with a sense of foreboding.

'He's just taking a phone call,' Lily said. 'Do you want me to—?' She didn't get any further as the door swung open and Razak strode into view, visibly upset.

'Ah, Mr Khan,' the administrator began immediately, obviously wanting to get his unpleasant task over as soon as possible. 'I'm sorry, but I'm afraid I've got some bad news. The contractor has just told me there's going to be a week's delay before the new theatre suite is ready for final inspection, and until then no operations can be scheduled…so your experiment will have to be delayed.'

'Mr Wardle, I can't tell you how delighted I am to hear that!' Razak exclaimed with an instant lightening of his expression, rendering the man completely speechless. 'I have just had a phone call to tell me that my father has collapsed and is in hospital. For my own peace of mind I need to visit him but I didn't see how this could be managed with completion so imminent. Now I can ask for everything to be delayed with a clear conscience. Yes?'

Lily's thoughts were in turmoil as she stood by silently, an unintentional witness to each announcement.

The news that the completion of the theatre suite was being delayed was annoying because they'd already begun to schedule staff, supplies and patients. It would be time-consuming to reorganise everything, to say nothing of the disappointment of the people who would now have another week or two of waiting and worrying before their suffering could be eased.

She empathised with Razak's need to visit his father. If it were hers, she would want to be there to see with her own eyes that he was recovering. It was pure serendipity that the disappointing delay would give Razak time to make his journey home, and the fact that her heart felt suddenly hollow at the thought that it could be a week before she saw him again was her own problem.

'When do you want to go? How long will you need to be away? Who will take over the care of your patients while you are away?' Ian demanded, the quick-fire list of questions showing the speed of his logical analysis of a situation that made him such an able administrator.

'My brother assures me that my father is out of surgery and is in as stable a condition as possible at present, but he is not a young man. Therefore, I would like to leave as soon as I can reschedule everything I have booked for the next week. I will brief Geoff Hargrave to take over the continuing care of our cases in my absence.'

That was a blow to Lily's ego—that her opposite number in Razak's firm was going to be given complete responsibility. But, then, he'd already been working here for six months and she'd arrived such a short time ago. She could hardly have expected anything else, no matter how well she and Razak had begun to work together.

'I would hope not to need to be away for more than three or four days, but for safety's sake…' He paused for a moment, as though making mental calculations, 'I would suggest that I sign myself out for exactly a week, then, if I arrive back sooner, I will be able to make myself available for any emergency admissions or I can use the time for administration in the run-up to the implementation of the new system.'

'Is there anything I can do to help?' Ian offered, the furrows in his forehead gradually smoothing out as his concerns were addressed so logically.

'I don't think so,' Razak said with a frown of his own. 'I must go and have a word with Mr Smythe in a moment to give him the bad news that the new theatre suite's completion has been delayed. At least I can also give him the good news that, as my list will be cancelled for a week, he is welcome to make use of my hours. Other than that… Oh, yes! There is something you could do. Could you authorise Dr Langley to be released from her hospital duties for a week?'

'*Me?* What…?' Up till that moment she might as well have been invisible for all the notice the two of them had taken of her. Suddenly she was the focus of both pairs of eyes.

'The two of us have been working together on a number of the logistical problems involved with the dual theatre system,' Razak continued swiftly, cutting into any objections she might have made. 'Also, while the changes were in the planning stages, I had a number of long meetings with

Geoff so he already knows exactly what the new system will involve. There has been no such time with Dr Langley because she arrived so recently.'

'But…' She must be missing something here. What difference would it make if she had to take a week off work if he was going to be out of the country?

'Also,' Razak continued in a more confidential tone, clearly unwilling for his next comments to be overheard by anyone outside their small group. 'There is the matter of Mr Smythe's antipathy towards female surgeons and the fact that if she were left to his tender mercies in my absence, she would be quite likely to spend the whole week twiddling her thumbs, shuffling papers and making tea.'

Ian gave a swiftly stifled snort of laughter in response to Razak's accurate assessment of the possibility then agreed readily to his request.

Lily was stunned by the speed of events as she watched the administrator hurry away from them, back to his own domain.

'So, Jazz, you are not angry with me?' Razak asked, with the first hint of uncertainty she'd ever seen in him.

Was she angry with him? Hardly, when she had no idea exactly what he had just let her in for.

'Should I be?' she countered. 'You asked for me to be released from my hospital duties but I've no idea what I *will* be doing. Acting as some sort of liaison while you're away? That's hardly—'

'Ah, no, Jazz. I see you have completely misunderstood. You will be coming *with* me while I visit my country.'

Lily hoped she wasn't standing there with her mouth open because she definitely felt as if she was gaping with surprise.

He wanted her to go with him? To travel with him to his country while he visited his father?

Those dark eyes were as intent as ever and once more she had the uncanny feeling that he could read every one of her thoughts.

'And did you think to ask if I have a passport before you organised my life?' she challenged softly, nearly chuckling aloud when he looked almost crestfallen. She'd been quite depressed at the thought of all the wheel-spinning she would have to do in the week he was away. This would be far more exciting, to say nothing of the fact that she would be spending so much time with him.

'I didn't think of that,' he admitted, pulling a wry face. 'I just had the sudden thought that if you were to come with me, not only would we be able to double-check all the arrangements for the new system and get to know each other better but I would also be able to show you the new facility where I'll be working when I come to the end of my contract here.'

Lily forced herself to ignore the pang of regret that he'd be leaving all too soon and concentrated instead on making the most of the time she would spend with him in the meantime.

'So, how long do you think it will take to do all the rescheduling and to brief Geoff about the present case load? Will I have time to go home and grab my toothbrush before we go to the airport?'

Watching the smile spread across his face as her words registered was almost like watching the sun come up.

'Certainly, we will have time to collect your toothbrush. And don't forget to collect your passport at the same time.'

The door swung open behind them and one of the nurses stuck her head out into the corridor.

'Are you ready to begin scrubbing?' she asked. 'Tim says your next patient's all checked, sedated and positioned and ready for the knife as soon as you like.'

'In that case, tell him we're on our way,' Razak advised crisply. 'We just need to scrub and we'll join him.' He turned to lead the way towards the small tiled anteroom with the stainless-steel sinks, glancing briefly over his shoulder to ask, 'So, Jazz, are you ready for the next one?'

'Which one is it first? The keyhole arthroscopy to remove the joint mouse or the torn cruciate ligament?' she asked, trying to sound businesslike as she followed his long-legged stride, hoping that her voice didn't give away just how euphoric she was feeling at the prospect of their trip together. If she was going to be able to keep her mind on the task ahead she was going to have to find a way to ignore the feeling of warmth that spread through her each time he called her Jazz in that husky voice. It would be far too easy to imagine that same voice speaking to her in just that way in far more intimate surroundings, and this was no time for impossible daydreams.

And, anyway, she reminded herself sternly as she rinsed the soap off her hands, careful as ever to make certain that the water drained from fingertip to elbow, she still had a long hard hill to climb before she reached her goal. She had no time to even think about sexy consultants with voices that sent a shiver of arousal right through her body.

Lily was delighted when Razak stepped back during the first operation, allowing her to lead as she probed the patient's knee for the chip of bone that periodically slid between the surfaces of the joint and prevented him from 'locking' the knee to stand and walk.

She was well aware that the view she had down the microscope was being shown simultaneously on a monitor so that Razak could follow what she was seeing and doing. All the time she was expecting him to speak up and offer appropriate advice and criticism, the way her previous mentor had, but when he remained completely silent she found it surprisingly easy to concentrate on what she was doing in spite of the fact that he was standing so close. There was actually a strange sense of security to know that he was there, rather than a feeling of threat that some hypercritical surgeons projected.

Although the second patient's symptoms were similar to the first, the cause was a little more complicated, with a torn section of the cruciate ligament causing the pain and disability. It took several minutes of fiddly snipping and meticulous retrieval of all the extraneous tissue before she was able to withdraw, ready to close her incisions.

'Jazz, I could not have done those procedures any better myself,' Razak announced to the room at large, and Lily's heart felt as if it turned a complete somersault in her chest at his praise. 'If you are quite happy to finish in here, I will go to my office and start on my phone calls.'

Lily murmured her agreement but as the doors swung closed behind him, out of the corner of her eye she saw one of the nurses nudge the other and lean close enough to whisper something that had the two of them staring in her direction.

So, the gossip was beginning.

Well, what had she expected? she mused as she positioned the second set of sutures. There had been an understandable groan of disappointment when Razak had entered the theatre after his conversation with the hospital administrator and broken the news about the delay in the completion of the new theatre suite. There had been an audible gasp of shock from several of the theatre staff when he'd followed that with the announcement that Lily would be accompanying him when he flew home to visit his father in hospital.

For a moment she thought about saying something but quickly realised that there was nothing she could say that would stop people from thinking what they wanted. How could they fail to be excited by the juicy titbit that the orthopaedic department's newest surgeon was going away for a week with its sexiest consultant?

She sighed silently and bit her tongue as she left to strip out of her disposables, glad she could appreciate the irony that the one person who had never done anything gossip-worthy had hit the jackpot without even trying. Thank goodness the whole department knew that the man wasn't married. At least she wouldn't be branded as a home-wrecker.

CHAPTER SIX

'JUST a minute, Khan!' Reg called across the room as Razak scooped the pile of letters out of his pigeonhole and turned to leave the room again. He muttered something uncomplimentary about the man's ancestry under his breath, grateful that it was in a dialect that few would understand even in his own country, and turned back to face Reg.

He'd hoped that Ian might have had time to tell the department head about the recent developments and was trying to find a polite way to tell Reg that he really didn't have the time, energy or inclination for another lengthy round of recriminations, but Reg beat him to it.

'Before you go sloping off for the day, there are a few things we need to get straight as soon as possible with those new theatres coming into action in the next few days. I'm going to be far too busy to talk in the morning and tomorrow afternoon I've got a full session of private patients, so—'

'I'm sorry, sir. I thought Mr Eardle might have told you,' Razak interrupted, politeness itself. 'My father has been taken ill and I will be travelling out to see him in the hospital. So I will not be free for a conversation tomorrow either.'

'But...what about the new theatre suite?' Reg demanded,

scandalised. 'You must be here to start work when it's commissioned. The hospital is arranging for one of the Royals to do some sort of opening ceremony and it would look pretty stupid to do it without the surgeon ready to—'

'I'm sorry, sir,' Razak interrupted again, fighting a grin. The whole department had heard little else than the fact that Reg would, of course, be the one to escort their exalted guest on the day. Razak had completely forgotten that the date and all the arrangements would now have to be changed, and with the full diaries that most of the members of the royal family maintained, it was unlikely that they would be able to accommodate the hospital. Poor Reg would not be happy to have his moment in the limelight spoiled. 'The completion date has been extended by a week due to unforeseen circumstances. I will definitely be back in time for the new opening ceremony.'

'What? Why wasn't I told?' he demanded, instantly incensed at the slight on his seniority.

'Possibly because you were busy in Theatre when the contractor told the hospital administrators?' Razak suggested. 'There will probably be a memo about it in your pigeonhole.'

'But…' For several seconds Reg's mouth worked without a sound coming out of it, as if he had no idea which tack to take. Unfortunately that state of affairs didn't last. 'I still have to decide about the allocation of hours in Theatre,' he declared pompously. 'We all have patients on our waiting lists, and we need to know when they can be called for admission.'

'Well, I've notified Administration that I'll be out of Theatre for the next week, so you're welcome to appropriate my hours as you see fit,' Razak offered, unsurprised to see the gleam in the head of department's eyes that told him he was thinking about the number of private patients he would be able to squeeze in. 'As for the new suite, initially I will be working one day a week for a five-hour stretch, using the two theatres simultaneously. Of course, the higher number of operations will mean that my consultation hours will be correspondingly greater, as will my follow-ups, so decisions about adding any extra theatre sessions will come later.'

'So you—'

'Of course,' Razak continued hurriedly, conscious that he had far too much to do before he needed to leave for the airport to stand there, debating. 'That does mean that I won't be taking up any time at all in the existing theatres unless I'm called on for an emergency outside my usual shifts, so you can allocate those hours as you please.'

He could almost hear the man doing the mathematics in his head. Razak was proposing an allocation of ten hours of theatre time divided between the two new theatres simultaneously. The other surgeons were each allocated three operating sessions per week, each session lasting for three and a half hours.

'That would seem to be satisfactory.' Reg nodded, apparently pleased that the rest of the surgeons would actually have half an hour each more than the upstart who wanted to try to teach them how to do their job.

'I'm glad you approve,' Razak said blandly, keeping to himself the thought that he was going to enjoy seeing that smug expression change once he had the new system up and running. 'Now, I do not wish to seem abrupt, but I have a flight to catch in a little more than three hours and much more to do before I can leave for the airport.'

In actual fact, he had done nearly everything on his list, the most time-consuming being the personal phone call he'd made to each of the patients who'd been booked for their operations in the coming week.

Several of them had been understandably upset, even angry, to learn that their long-awaited surgery was being postponed at this late date. He'd deliberately told each one of them that, rather than it being the fault of the hospital, it was his own personal circumstances that were dictating the delay. He'd been quite touched by how understanding most people were when they heard about his father's illness and he'd promised each of them that they would hear from him again to reschedule their operation as soon as he returned.

Now there was just one more visit that he wanted to make before he would feel easy in his mind, and that was to the men's surgical ward.

'Mr Bullen?' he said softly when he arrived in the man's room and found him with his eyes closed. They flickered once then opened.

'Oh. It's you,' Simon rasped in a voice that still sounded raw as a result of the trauma to his throat.

'I just came to see if you were all right. I'll be away for a few days.'

'Holiday? Exotic destination, I bet,' he said, with an attempt at a sneer.

'Exotic destination, yes, but it won't be a holiday. My father's collapsed and been taken into hospital for heart surgery,' Razak said, wondering how on earth he was going to get through to this man. On the surface they had absolutely nothing in common but there was something about him that...

'I'm sorry,' Simon said quietly, and had the grace to look a little shamefaced. 'Are you close?'

'Yes and no.' He smiled wryly. 'Both he and my mother wanted me to…to go into the family business. *I* wanted to be a doctor. I don't think they're ever going to give up trying to change my mind.'

'Wish I'd had your courage,' Simon said suddenly, and just like that a connection had been forged between them. 'I wanted to be a musician…apparently I was damn good, too. But I took over the family business because music's not a job for a man who wants a wife and family…' Tears welled in his bloodshot eyes. 'So I end up with nothing. No music, no wife, no family, no business…'

Razak wordlessly pushed the box of tissues within reach of the man's good arm and held it so that he could pull several out. He let the silence stretch out for a while before he spoke, unexpectedly knowing something of what the man must have been feeling when he'd resorted to such a drastic step.

'So you know what it feels like to be backed into a corner with no way out,' he mused softly. 'And all you can think about is all the things you could have done if only… And then you feel so ungrateful because even though you want things to be different, there is so much that is good about your life. There's your family, the roof over your head, a job that lets you put food on the table…'

'But all the time you know that there's something missing,' his patient said with an edge of despair. 'That your life's not…not what it *could* have been.'

'So, one day, everything changes…' Razak hinted, hoping that it would keep him talking.

'One day I realised that I was still backed into the same corner and all I had time to do was work. So my wife was bored with me and found a newer, richer model but still she wants half of everything that's left…the house, the business…'

'And you were so depressed that you didn't realise that you'd been looking at everything the wrong way, focussing on the wrong things and not letting yourself look outside the box. So you didn't even realise that she was giving you a second chance,' Razak suggested, suddenly seeing other tenuous parallels with his own situation.

'Second chance?' Simon scoffed. 'No way! She's filed for divorce.'

'Exactly!' Razak grinned at him as he leaned forward in the chair to make his point. 'She's giving you a second chance to do what you really want to do with your life, without the responsibility of putting a roof over *her* head and food on *her* table…if you still want to do it.'

This time he was determined not to be the one to break the silence but his thoughts took him down pathways of their own.

'Sometimes…' Razak mused, staring down at the hands that were so much more fulfilled when they were solving other people's surgical needs than they ever would their financial or political requirements. He knew that he had made the right choice of career, but… 'Sometimes, other people can see more than you can about your own life, and it is wonderful if they can point you in the right direction, but sometimes they are more interested in their own wishes and will try to force you into being something that will never make you happy.'

'The trouble is, you can be up to your neck in doing things to make other people happy before you realise everything's gone wrong,' Simon rasped. 'And you can't see any way of making it right.'

'So maybe you should take a step back and work out if you really *want* to make it right, or if it is the time to draw a line under it and start afresh.'

'Easy to say,' Simon said grimly. 'Not so easy to do with mortgage arrears piling up and a business falling apart.'

'So, decide what's important to you—hanging onto the remnants of your past life or getting rid of the chains. Then decide how you're going to go about getting the life you really want.'

This time he managed to let the silence stretch out until his patient broke it, but in that time he'd seen a complete transformation in the expression in his eyes.

'Or,' Simon said slowly, as though working out his words as the thoughts evolved, 'I could put my shoulder to the wheel just long enough to get my finances straight…then sell it all for as much as I can get, so I pay my wife off to get rid of her once and for all. Then I can be who I really wanted to be…

'Hell, who am I kidding?' he growled. 'I'm never going to be a star at my age, no matter how good my songs are.'

'I don't see that age stopped anyone listening to Sinatra or the Rolling Stones and you're a good deal younger than Pavarotti. Anyway, who said you have to be the singer? There are a lot of those about, but not nearly so many who can write their own songs,' Razak pointed out, wishing he knew a little more about the business so he could be more help.

The alarm he'd set on his mobile phone started to bleep, reminding him that he still had a flight to catch.

'I'm sorry but I must go now or I will miss my flight,' he

apologised, but he had a feeling that the man lying there with injuries from top to bottom barely heard him for the thoughts going round inside his head. 'I will see you when I return,' he promised, and turned to find Lily leaning against the doorframe and looking as if she'd been there for some time.

He found himself trying to replay what he'd said to their patient and wondering how much he'd given away. Had he made it obvious that he'd been thinking about her and the way she'd burst into his life like a ray of sunshine when all he'd been able to see ahead had been a monochromatic world of work and more work while his emotional life withered away completely?

'Ready to go?' she asked as she led the way down the corridor, a neat carry-on bag in her hand.

'How far away do you live and how long will it take you to pack when we get there?' he asked as he breathed a sigh of relief.

'Already done,' she said with a gesture towards the bag in her hand.

'Is that all you're taking?' he demanded in amazement. 'My sisters would need more than that to go away for a single night. For a week they would need a mountain of suitcases.'

'I don't really have much in my wardrobe suitable for your part of the world, so I just packed lightweight trousers and tops with long sleeves with a pashmina in case it gets cool in the evening.'

Razak's regard for his new junior reached new heights. A woman who could manage to find time to pack somewhere in the middle of a busy day and without taking everything she possessed with her was a rarity indeed. He was just as lightly laden—there was little point in taking much with him when there was a complete set of belongings waiting for him in the family home.

'Well, if you've got your passport in there, too, we can get off to the airport. The plane will be waiting for us.'

The plane will be waiting for us, he'd said, and Lily had chuckled at the very idea. She'd only discovered that he'd been speaking the literal truth when they were shown to a large executive jet with a discreet crest on the fuselage.

So, here she was ensconced in the unimaginable luxury of butter-soft leather seats in a room that looked as if it belonged in an upmarket hotel rather than the cabin of an aircraft.

'Does your father have important friends?' she asked weakly as he ushered her inside and made sure she was comfortable before taking the seat beside her.

'Several,' he said cryptically, the word almost lost in the sudden surge of sound from the jets that was apparently the result of his seat belt clicking shut. Within seconds, it seemed, they were racing along the runway and were airborne.

'Would you like something to eat or would you rather sleep first?' Razak asked once they were in level flight and a young steward came to stand at his elbow. 'Even in this plane we will be in the air for about five hours and with the change in time zones it will be early morning when we arrive.'

Disorientation was setting in. Lily had been expecting the usual lengthy check-in and wait at the airport but somehow they'd been whisked through like royalty and ushered onto a plane that looked like something out of a magazine article on the lives of the rich and famous.

Now, instead of an arbitrary timetable dictating when she should be fed from a plastic tray, she was being offered a choice of whether to eat now or later.

The steward held out a menu and her first glance had her stomach rumbling noisily.

Razak laughed sympathetically. 'Me, too!' he said. 'Neither of us stopped for food today, by the sound of it. What would you like?'

Salmon, chicken or steak? They all looked delicious when she was so hungry.

'How about sharing some salmon as a starter then having chicken or steak for a main course?' he suggested, when she couldn't decide.

'In that case, yes, please, and I'd like the chicken,' she said with a grateful smile. 'But how I'll ever be able to make a decision about dessert, with so many delicious options on the menu, I don't know. Look at it…*crème brûlée*, profiteroles, lemon posset *and* death by chocolate! It's as if someone peeped inside my head and found out all my favourites!'

There was a strange gleam in his eye for a second and she remembered a conversation one day when the two of them had finished surgery too late for anything but a very tired, leathery piece of apple pie. They'd discussed their favourite menus that day, but it must just be an amazing coincidence that several of her choices were on the menu today…surely?

Then their poached salmon starter arrived on its bed of frilly lettuce and there was no more time for thought, just blissful tasting of succulent fish seasoned and cooked to perfection, followed by an equally delicious breast of chicken that had been butterflied and pan-fried and was served with a creamy sauce and a selection of baby vegetables.

When it was time for dessert the young steward approached with the menu again but Razak held up his hand and quickly said something in his own language.

'What did you tell him?' Lily demanded, when the young man went off with a grin on his face.

'Wait and see,' Razak said with a grin of his own that had her pulse clamouring for something far more potent than even her favourite desserts.

In spite of the fact that they were on their way to visit his father and that the man was apparently seriously ill, she didn't think she'd ever seen Razak looking so relaxed. It made her realise just how much stress he must be under with the whole weight of responsibility for the success of this controversial trial on his shoulders.

'Madam?' said a voice beside her shoulder, and it was the steward offering her a plate crammed with an almost full portion of *each* dessert on the menu.

'Razak!' she exclaimed through a gurgle of laughter, suddenly realising what he must have told the young man to do. 'I can't possibly eat all this!'

'Then you'll just have to share,' he said smugly, as he grabbed his spoon.

For a moment she fended him off as though jealously guarding a treasure then she realised that these moments of nonsense were making her feel more carefree than she could ever remember. For the first time in many years she was actually having fun.

Razak, too, seemed unusually light-hearted while they argued over the fair distribution of the spoils and she wondered whether this was usually a feature of his off-duty persona. Apart from her unexpected attraction to him…attraction that had been growing stronger from the first day she'd met him…she really knew so little about him other than his role as a surgeon and her mentor.

There were so many things she wanted to ask him—about his family, his country, his aspirations about the job he was looking forward to so much when his contract ended—but almost as soon as she'd finished the last delicious mouthful of her share she felt her eyelids growing heavy and the next thing she knew was Razak's hand gently shaking her shoulder.

'Lily?' he murmured, that husky voice so close to her ear that she could feel the warmth of his breath on the side of her face. 'It is time.'

'Time?' She opened her eyes lazily as the lingering remnants of a dream blurred the fiction of the two of them sharing a bed with the reality of finding those dark, dark eyes so close that she could have counted every one of his eyelashes.

'Time to do up your seat belt,' he explained, as he straightened away from her and settled himself in his own seat. 'We will be landing in a few minutes.'

Lily turned her face away from him and busied herself searching for the two ends of the belt, hoping that he couldn't see the sudden surge of colour in her cheeks.

Seeing him there so close to her had been so much like her dream that she'd almost offered her mouth for the kiss he'd been about to give her in her sleep. How embarrassing it would have been if he'd realised just how much she'd wanted to feel his lips on hers, and how inappropriate. Apart from the fact that he was her boss, she was far too ordinary for someone as handsome as Razak.

She thought she'd got herself under control by the time they stepped out into the building heat of a brilliant new day when she saw the gleaming limousine waiting for them at the bottom of the steps.

'Razak?' she began uncertainly, when the driver hurried to open the door for them with what sounded like a formal salutation.

'Please, make yourself comfortable,' Razak said, his accent sounding more pronounced and sexier than ever now that he was surrounded by his countrymen. 'If it is all right with you, we will drive straight to the hospital.'

'At this hour of the morning?' she exclaimed. 'Can you imagine what the staff in CICU would say if visitors turned up so early?'

'I don't think the hour of our visit will cause a problem,' he said confidently, and the penny dropped.

'Ah, is that because this is the hospital where you're going to be working when you return home? Are they already according you staff privileges?'

'Something like that,' he agreed, as they swept regally through a hospital entrance that couldn't be any more different from the inner-city one where they worked together, flanked as it was by the towering trunks of palm trees.

There was a very nervous-looking gentleman waiting for them at the entrance of the cardiac unit who looked as if he'd rather be *anywhere* else. It didn't take Razak long to have him smiling and eager to take them to visit his patient.

In deference to his father's privacy Lily intended waiting in the corridor but Razak left her no option when he placed a courteous hand at the back of her waist to usher her into the high-tech room.

She could see at once where Razak had inherited his looks, although the elderly man connected to all the wires and tubes looked desperately frail—that was, right up to the moment when Razak introduced her and he turned those dark eyes on her.

For the first time in her life, Lily had a feeling she knew what it would feel like to be a specimen under a microscope. It couldn't be any less intense than the way his father examined her from head to toe and back again to focus on her face.

Lily had always known that she hadn't inherited any of the family's beauty but she didn't think she had anything to be apologetic about with her academic achievements. When his imperious glare seemed to go on far longer than politeness permitted, her chin came up a belligerent inch and she was startled to see an answering gleam of humour in his eyes. The old man threw a brief husky sentence at his son before he raised a heavily veined hand and waved them both closer.

'So, you work together?' he said, his hand holding tightly to Razak's as if it were a lifeline.

'Lily is a junior surgeon on my team,' Razak said, but those old eyes were fixed on her again.

'And are you a *good* surgeon?' he challenged her directly.

'Not as good as I *will* be,' she said firmly, feeling almost as if she was going through an unexpected job interview.

This time he actually laughed, the sound weak and papery but enough to make her feel as euphoric as if she'd somehow passed an important test.

'Rest, Father,' Razak counselled gently. 'I will come back later.'

'Bring her with you,' he ordered weakly, as tiredness overcame him and closed his eyes. 'Bring Lily.'

Razak seemed utterly drained by the time they returned to the waiting limousine. He hadn't slept when she had on the flight if the briefcase full of papers he'd brought with him was any indication...but she could also see his relief at the cardiologist's report that the condition of his father's heart condition wasn't as bad as he'd feared. Where once his general health would have prevented him from having the open-heart surgery his condition required, the latest developments in the design of stents meant that the same outcome that would have been achieved from coronary bypass surgery had been achieved with a procedure that was less stressful than balloon angioplasty.

'Finally, it's time to go home,' he murmured, as he rested his head back against the supple leather. 'Soon we will be able to take a shower and relax.'

Lily took advantage of the fact that his eyes were closed to look at him without the fear that he would catch her doing it.

With a grimace at the unfairness of life she noted that while she looked thoroughly wilted, he looked barely rumpled in his elegantly tailored suit. There were shadows under his eyes that were only partly hidden by those ridiculously long lashes and his hair was rumpled, but otherwise no one would have known that this was the first time he'd really relaxed in nearly twenty-four hours.

Far too soon they were turning in through an ornate gateway and their chauffeur said something that opened Razak's eyes and had him straightening up in his seat.

Lily had a strong suspicion that their driver had somehow notified their destination that they were near because by the time the vehicle glided to a halt in front of the massive doors in the middle of the imposing white façade there seemed to be nearly a dozen people gathered to welcome Razak home.

She barely stifled a chuckle when she realised that most of them were staff who had apparently been detailed to carry their luggage for them, only to find a single small case apiece and Razak's briefcase when they opened up the back of the vehicle.

'Come inside out of the heat,' Razak invited, and Lily was grateful for the suggestion. The sun had grown so much hotter in the brief time they had been in the hospital that it felt hard to breathe and her shirt was now sticking uncomfortably to her back.

She had hoped that she would avoid meeting any more people until she'd had a chance to freshen up, but as soon as her eyes grew accustomed to the comparative darkness of the lofty pillared hallway she could see another group of people approaching them.

Razak exclaimed aloud and strode swiftly forward to embrace the elegant older woman of the group, before gesturing Lily forward.

'Lily, this is my mother,' he announced with a smile, and Lily found herself looking down into eyes filled with blatant suspicion that bordered on dislike. 'Mother,' he continued, apparently oblivious to what was going on right under his aristocratic nose, 'this is Dr Lily Langley. She is a colleague of mine and a gifted surgeon.'

Wordlessly, his mother accorded Lily the briefest nod of acknowledgement before turning back to her son.

Although she didn't understand a single word, Lily could tell that his mother was angry with him and felt embarrassed that *she* was obviously the cause of her displeasure. Was it because she felt it inappropriate for him to have brought a visitor with him while his father was ill? Or perhaps it was because it was obvious that Lily plainly didn't belong in such sumptuous surroundings. She'd certainly never been in anywhere as luxurious since she'd taken advantage of a guided tour round one of the stately homes in England.

'Enough, Mother,' Razak said impatiently, but he was gentle as he removed the hand clutching tightly at his arm. 'We worked all day yesterday and travelled for most of the night. We need to go to our rooms.'

His mother beckoned a young woman forward with a single sentence but Razak swiftly countermanded her.

'I will show Lily to her rooms,' he said. 'We will probably sleep for a while but if you send someone to wake us, we will join you for the midday meal.'

Razak could have chosen his words better, Lily thought when she realised that it sounded almost as though the two of them would be sleeping together. Then she saw the expression of shock on his mother's face and realised that was exactly the way *she'd* understood them, too, and with a stab of dismay suddenly realised that the older woman had deliberately erected a language barrier between them so that she didn't have to speak directly to her.

That insight totally robbed her of words as she followed meekly in Razak's wake, his long strides taking him out of the palatial entrance and into the first of a series of imposing corridors.

Suddenly, without any warning, he stopped in his tracks and she barely avoided ploughing into his back.

'I apologise,' he said tightly, his mouth pressed into an angry line.

'I should have been watching where I was going,' she said uncertainly, not recognising his mood. He wasn't an easy man to read, keeping most of his thoughts to himself, but she'd never seen him quite this agitated.

'I didn't mean…' He shook his head and began again. 'I apologise for my mother and the way…' A sudden noise at the other end of the corridor had him breaking off again with what could only be a muttered imprecation under his breath.

'Come. We cannot speak here,' he announced, and strode away again, this time so swiftly that she was almost forced to run to keep up.

The last thing she needed was to lose him, she thought with a hint of hysteria. This place was so vast that she might never be seen again…which would probably please his mother no end, she added darkly to herself.

CHAPTER SEVEN

LILY was short of breath from keeping up with him by the time Razak finally paused in front of an imposing wooden door. When he threw it open to reveal a room that seemed filled with light in spite of the gauzy curtains drawn to filter the sunshine she could only gasp at its beauty.

The furniture was a clever mixture of old and new, traditional and modern, but it was the view outside that completely stole her breath.

'Oh, Razak, look!' she whispered, as a flicker of movement drew her eyes and she hurried across to draw one of the curtains aside. 'Did you see that?'

Outside, centred in the enclosed atrium surrounded by a traditional colonnade, was a stretch of glimmering water surrounded by cool blue and white patterned tiles. As she took in the profusion of plants that filled each corner, spilling out of every size and shape of container, another bird swooped down, leaving a sharp slash in the water's surface that widened into ripples.

'There's another one!' she exclaimed, and laughed in delight. 'What sort of bird is it and what are they doing?'

'I don't know what you would call them,' he admitted.

'But they are migrating birds that stop here briefly at this time each year when they are on their way north for the summer and then, later, when they make the return journey to escape the northern winter. Every year that I can remember at least some of them have found this water and performed this feat, scooping up beakfuls of water over and over to satisfy their thirst after the long journey across the desert.'

'They're beautiful!' she exclaimed, glancing back at him as he came to stand behind her and she moved to one side to give him room to watch with her. 'They're so swift and agile and…' Her words faded away when she realised that he wasn't looking at the birds at all but was gazing down at her, his dark eyes more intent than ever.

'What?' she demanded nervously, knowing that she looked far from her best after so many hours' travelling.

'Ah, Jazz, you are such a special person,' he said quietly, as he used a single fingertip to stroke several stray strands of hair away from her face.

She felt her eyes widen at the unexpected gesture, marvelling that something so simple could feel so much like a caress, and as for the intimacy of using the nickname he had chosen for her…

Before she could untangle her vocal cords long enough to protest that she wasn't special at all, just ordinary, very ordinary, he was speaking again.

'My mother was unforgivably rude to you when you arrived—rude to a guest I have brought to my home—but instead of taking offence, you find delight in watching birds drinking from a pool.'

She was completely lost for words. What could she say?

Tell him that she'd been hurt that his mother had realised at first glance that she was nowhere near their social standing? Hardly. It was nothing less than the truth and there was nothing she could do or say to make it any different.

At the same time Lily felt that she *should* say something, otherwise Razak's discomfort at his mother's discourtesy might colour her whole stay in his home.

'Razak, your mother has been desperately worried about your father and has probably slept even less than we have. How can I possibly take offence if she's less than totally welcoming to a stranger being foisted on her at such a time?'

He smiled down at her and shook his head. 'As I said, you are a special woman,' he whispered, and bent his head to brush the briefest of kisses across her lips.

Razak leant his forehead against the tiled wall and groaned as the cold water poured over his body.

It had been nearly half an hour since he'd made the crazy mistake of kissing Lily. At the time it had felt perfect and if she hadn't slapped his face for his presumption, he'd been fully prepared to make it the first of many, in spite of the fact he was so tired he could barely see straight. Then, out of the corner of his eye, he'd seen the curtains move in one of the rooms on the other side of the atrium and had realised that, with the curtain still pulled aside and clenched tight in Lily's hand, whoever was watching them had seen far more than he would have wished.

So here he was, standing under a cold shower wondering exactly how long it would be before news of his misdemeanour reached his mother.

The fact that he'd installed Lily in the suite right next

to his own was already making her unhappy, but there was no way he could have let his mother carry out her intention of banishing her to the far reaches of the guest wing all on her own, no matter how luxurious the accommodation was. Lily wasn't the sort of person to want to ring a bell every time she wanted directions, but without them most people would become lost in this vast warren. At least with her in the room beside his, he could escort her to where she needed to go.

It was nobody's business but his own that the decision had been anything but spur of the moment. He'd spent far too much of the flight watching her as she'd slept and planning to have her installed in the suite next to his. In all conscience he couldn't take his attraction any further than that single kiss, but that didn't mean he couldn't dream about it, especially when she'd seemed every bit as dissatisfied that he'd stopped as he had.

He groaned again at his body's predictable response and turned the water off, finally admitting that it wasn't going to do any good if he couldn't stop thinking about her, as well as being a waste of his country's precious resources.

No, instead of trying to forget how soft and sweet her lips had tasted, his time would be far better spent in concentrating on what he would say if…no, make that *when*…his mother confronted him with his transgression. Or, better yet, he should be organising to visit the hospital again to see how much progress had been made on the construction of the new dedicated orthopaedic surgery department.

There was a sharp knock on his door just as he strode out of the bathroom and his sudden thought that Lily might walk in on him had an all too predictable effect on his naked body.

'Hey, big brother!' exclaimed Karim pointedly, as he let himself in without waiting for an invitation. Razak felt a juvenile blush work its way up his throat and into his face as he turned away to reach for a robe.

'To what do I owe the pleasure of your company?' he asked stiffly.

'It doesn't look as if it's the pleasure of *my* company that you want, Raz,' Karim teased, as he dropped down to sprawl into the corner of a sofa. 'Do I take it you've heard that Mother-dear is trying to persuade Dita to come home for a visit?'

'But that is crazy when she has exams so soon!' Razak exclaimed. 'And it is a waste of time when I will be gone in a few days.'

'Then you are not so eager to see her that you will snatch at any chance?' Karim said with an innocent expression on his face. They both knew that he was goading, trying to get a reaction out of his big brother, and with a blinding flash of revelation Razak suddenly realised why.

Transfixed by his thoughts, he was still standing there trying to find the right words to voice the impossible when there was a second, more hesitant knock on the door.

Karim called out for whoever it was to enter and Razak's heart gave several extra beats when Lily's beautiful face peered hesitantly round the door.

Once more his body threatened to embarrass him and with a muttered apology he hurried back towards the bathroom, only remembering to scoop up an armful of clothing at the last minute.

Lily couldn't help the way her eyes followed Razak's broad back as he strode out of the room, admiring the way the heavy silk of his gown lovingly outlined it and the tight curves of his buttocks before tracing the length of dark hair-sprinkled muscular legs.

A stifled chuckle made her close her eyes in mortification that she'd been caught ogling the man. Running away to hide was an option, but it wasn't *her* way so she forced herself to meet dark eyes that were almost exactly like Razak's and gleaming with suppressed laughter.

'I am Karim,' he said, as he leapt up and strode across to her, taking her hand to pull her further into the room. 'I am Raz's younger and much more handsome brother.'

Lily couldn't help laughing. 'Younger? I will have to take your word on that, but much more handsome? Surely that is in the eye of the beholder?'

'And?' he challenged, striking a theatrical pose.

Lily put on a thoughtful expression as she examined him from top to toe then rocked her hand in an expression of uncertainty. It was his turn to laugh as the bathroom door opened and Razak emerged with a face like thunder.

'Don't you have any work to do?' he snapped, as he retrieved his phone and a set of keys and slid them into his pocket. 'Lily and I don't have any time to waste. We have a meeting at the hospital with the architect.'

Lily blinked. The last she'd heard, the two of them were supposed to be catching up on some sleep. Now he was saying they had an immediate appointment? Then she caught an exchange of glances between the two brothers and realised there were deeper undercurrents in the room than she was privy to.

'Of course,' Karim agreed with barely concealed humour. 'You have an urgent meeting with the architect who was chosen specifically because you trusted him to complete the project in your absence.'

Karim was poking fun at his big brother, Lily realised, fascinated to see this glimpse into his private life. Was he taking advantage of the fact that she was there to prevent Razak retaliating? How deep *was* the rivalry between the two of them?

'And you doubtless have a mountain of work waiting for you on Father's desk. Are you ready to go, Lily?' Razak asked her briskly, and she glanced down at the white cotton trousers topped by a lightweight long-sleeved top covered in delicate swirls of green, blue and turquoise.

'Will this do, or am I dressed too casually?' she asked, suddenly uncomfortably aware that the wardrobe she'd brought with her might be woefully lacking. She certainly hadn't expected to be living in a house that was little less than a palace and to find that Razak had a seemingly inexhaustible supply of expensive suits.

'That will be perfect if it feels cool and comfortable,' he said, suddenly shrugging out of his jacket and depositing it on the arm of a nearby chair.

She saw Karim's eyebrows shoot up and wondered if this sudden informality was something new. She was accustomed to seeing Razak in suits or wilted theatre scrubs at the end of a hard operating session and knew that he lost none of his air of command whichever he wore.

Reassured that she wasn't dressed inappropriately and suddenly exhilarated that she was going to be spending the morning with Razak, Lily only just remembered to smile in Karim's direction and utter an anodyne 'Nice to have met you' before she allowed Razak to usher her out of the door.

'Raz?' he called, and they both paused while Karim met

his brother's eyes and gave him a smiling nod. 'Now I understand,' he said, almost too softly for her to hear, casting a fleeting glance in Lily's direction.

Razak frowned heavily for a second and started to shake his head before he gave a rueful grin and a nod. 'Well, then, little brother, see that you take advantage of the situation as soon as possible.'

Lily couldn't make head or tail of the exchange, but whatever they'd been talking about seemed to have had an amazing effect on Razak's disposition.

Ever since they'd entered those imposing doors he'd been filled with so much tension that the air had almost crackled around him.

By the time he'd led the way out of a side exit and waved away the chauffeur-driven limousine in favour of a nondescript dust-covered car that he drove himself, he was actually humming under his breath with a half-smile curving the corners of his mouth.

Finally, knowing that she couldn't face a near-silent journey when she was filled with too many questions to bear, she tried to find an innocuous topic of conversation.

'What is the difference in age between you and Karim?' she asked, still amazed by the fact that two brothers could look so alike and yet she had absolutely no reaction to one while every cell in her body quivered when she so much as thought about the other.

There was a pause before he answered, almost as if he was waiting to pull up at the traffic light ahead before speaking.

'Six months,' he said quietly, and even behind the dark lenses of his sunglasses she could see that he was watching her startled reaction.

'Six?' she repeated faintly, for a moment unable to untangle the logistics.

'We had different mothers,' he said, just as she'd come to that conclusion by a process of deduction. 'Leila was our father's second wife and died shortly after Karim was born...possibly of some form of post-partum sepsis, reading between the lines, but these things are not discussed with the men of the family, even if they've become doctors. Thankfully, such things are rare these days. We have a programme of tuition for the traditional healers in the more remote regions so that their patients can have the best of both systems...the village midwife to attend them for straightforward deliveries and hospital treatment available in case of complications.'

One part of her brain was absorbing the information about his country's health-care system while the other part was still reeling with aftershocks from his unexpected revelation. She'd known that for many countries in this part of the world plural marriages were not only legal but the accepted norm.

'You find the idea repugnant?' he asked, and she was glad that the car was once more in motion and his eyes no longer tracking her every expression.

'Not repugnant in essence,' she said slowly, as she sifted through her chaotic thoughts and feelings. 'If it's a traditional part of a culture that both the men and the women are happy with, then my opinions are meaningless.'

'But?' he prompted, as though he knew without doubt that there was more. Sometimes she really did believe that he could read her mind.

'But it wouldn't work for me,' she said firmly.

'Because?' He really wasn't going to let this go, was he?

'Because, if…when I marry, it will be my first and last time and I will put everything of myself into that relationship with nothing left to share with anyone else. I will expect my husband to be prepared to put exactly the same degree of commitment into our union or there will be no marriage.'

'So certain and so adamant,' he murmured, as he made the final turn into the hospital grounds before veering onto something that was little more than an unmade track that led around to the rear of the imposing building.

'You disagree?' she challenged, with a sudden feeling of disappointment and a realisation of just how little she knew about this man. 'You would prefer to have several wives at your beck and call?'

'In a way, the idea is attractive,' he said in a musing tone. 'Imagine having four wives, each vying to please me the most. But, on the other hand, imagine having four mothers-in-law.' He gave a theatrical shudder. 'Uh-uh! Not for me, thanks!'

She saw him throw her a sideways glance as though he was assessing her response and deliberately tried to keep her expression neutral. He'd made a joke of it but there was a profound principle at the heart if it.

The silence stretched for several heartbeats as he parked and switched off the engine, then he turned towards her and took his sunglasses off to fix her with a totally serious gaze.

'All joking aside, when I get married, I too would want it to be for life to a woman who loves me as much as I love her. One wife, one marriage.'

And if she hadn't been sitting down she would have melted into a puddle at his feet with the effect of the sincerity in those dark eyes. As it was, she was in danger of hyperventilating as she imagined being the focus of that intensity for the rest of her life and didn't even notice that he'd left the vehicle and walked around to open the door for her until she nearly fell out of the car.

'Sorry…must have dozed off for a second,' she mumbled as she scrambled to her feet. 'What exactly are we doing here?' Had they travelled thousands of miles only to replace one building site with another?

'This,' he said, with a wide gesture of one shirt-clad arm, 'will eventually be a specialist orthopaedic surgery department. Right from the first day it will be run so that all the surgeons who work here will make the most effective use of their time by utilising two theatres in series.'

'Exactly the same as you're going to do as soon as *our* new theatre suite is finished,' she said with a grin. 'How many theatres will there be in total? How many surgeons will the hospital have on staff and what about the anaesthetists and the other theatre staff and—?'

She hadn't even finished asking her questions let alone given him a chance to answer before a gentleman with a builder's hard hat shouted across to them and beckoned.

The next hour was fascinating as the architect showed her the blueprints for the facility he called Razak's baby, at the same time as he reassured the man himself that everything was proceeding to plan.

'In fact, if work continues at this pace, there is even a chance that it will be completed early,' he said with a broad grin lifting the ends of his impressive moustache. 'So many of the men working on it have relatives who need to come here for operations that they can't wait to see it finished. Some of them are even volunteering to work overtime for the basic rate of pay!'

Their progress meeting over, Razak led the way into the cardiac unit to visit his father again before he returned home.

'Come in! Come in!' He beckoned when Lily remained outside to give the two men some privacy. 'You are a doctor, too? Yes?'

'Yes, sir. An orthopaedic surgeon, like your son,' she explained, but he waved that aside.

'But you know how to read a patient's chart,' he demanded with a touch of impatience.

'Of course, sir,' she agreed, wondering exactly where he was going with this. 'We all have to be able to do that.'

'Even orthopaedic surgeons?'

'Even orthopaedic surgeons, yes.'

'Then can you tell me why my son is unable to read my chart to tell me whether my operation has been a success and how long I have to stay in here before I can go home again?'

'Father…!' Razak said in a warning tone, but Lily didn't need him to intervene. After so many years of medical training she had some of her answers off pat, having heard the questions so many times.

'Of course I can tell you why,' she replied smartly, even as she silently applauded the wily old man for his attempt at manipulating both of them.

'You can?' he said slightly taken aback. 'Then why?'

'It's only a couple of little things called professional courtesy and medical ethics. Not terribly important to some people, but they help to keep the rest of us on the straight and narrow.'

Razak burst out laughing at his father's disgusted expression. 'I think you've met your match,' he said. 'You're just going to have to be patient.'

'But you come home so rarely these days, and I am not

there to see you,' he complained, holding out his hand towards his son.

Lily felt her eyes grow moist when she saw the careful way Razak cradled his father's hand between his own.

'Don't you try using emotional blackmail on me,' he chided gently. 'This visit is just a bonus. If you hadn't needed to come into hospital, you probably wouldn't have seen me at all until I finished my contract in England. The new theatre suite there is almost finished and within the next couple of weeks Jazz and I will be operating in it, using the new system.'

'This is good, my son. You will need the experience if you are to be able to take on… *Jazz*?' he echoed with a frown as the nickname registered. 'But you told me the young lady's name is Lily.'

'It's because of the music,' Lily said hastily, suddenly uncomfortable with the idea that Razak might mention the more intimate reason he'd given her the nickname. 'When we're operating, we take it in turns to choose the music that's playing.'

'And you choose jazz,' he said with a smile of comprehension.

'And sometimes blues, especially on the saxophone,' she added. 'I find it helps me to concentrate…not be distracted by the other things that are going on around me in the operating theatre.'

She was uncomfortably aware that she'd begun to babble, but his eyes were so like his son's and it was almost as if he knew that she was having to fight her need to look at the man standing so close beside her. She could feel the warmth of his body through the fine fabric of her sleeve and smell the fresh clean scent of soap from his skin and all she could think about was the way that heavy silk robe had flowed over him to tell her that he was completely naked underneath it.

'I like you,' the old man said suddenly. 'Come back and visit me again, if you want to.'

'I would like that,' she said. 'But I don't know how much time we'll have as Razak has brought a great deal of paperwork with him to do with the new system he's introducing.'

'So, come without him,' he suggested, and it was almost a challenge, as if he was testing her nerve.

'I will,' she said, and this time didn't bother trying to hide her smile, letting him know that she'd accepted the challenge.

A nurse bustled in, pushing a drugs trolley that could have been the twin of the one in their own surgical wards, and Razak took advantage of the interruption to take their leave.

'I'm sorry, Jazz, but by the time we drive home, we will be too late to join the family for the midday meal,' he apologized, as he led the way back out into the enervating heat to go to the car. 'Would you like to get something to eat in a restaurant? You have seen nothing of the city yet.'

Lily certainly wasn't sorry to have missed another chance to be glared at by Razak's mother. His father had been far more welcoming.

'Is it all right…?' She hesitated, not wanting to cause offence. 'Is it permissible for the two of us to have a meal together…in public? It won't cause a problem…a scandal for your family?'

'Not so long ago, it might have,' he agreed, gesturing for her to wait a moment or two for the air-conditioning in the car to lower the temperature before she got in. 'But these days a substantial part of the country's income is from tourism, so this has had to change. Still, the traditionalists appreciate it when people avoid…flaunting? No, this is not exactly…'

'You mean, when people avoid showing too much flesh in public—stick to long sleeves, for example,' she said, with a gesture towards her own attire as they settled themselves on the smooth leather seats. 'But that is just plain common sense for someone with skin as pale as mine.'

For just a second it was almost as if she could feel the touch of his eyes on the triangle of skin exposed at her throat before he replaced the sunglasses he'd taken off as he'd got into the car.

'Exactly,' he said in a voice that sounded slightly huskier than usual, then cleared his throat. 'But that doesn't answer the question of whether you would like to have a meal before we go back. I will even take you on a short guided tour of our fair city.'

Lily's spirits rose at the thought that their time together wasn't over yet, but when she tried to imagine herself walking around in this sort of heat she just couldn't face it.

'I'm sorry, but it's just too hot for sightseeing. I'm not used to this heat and—'

'Forgive me for my thoughtlessness,' he interrupted swiftly. 'And I was forgetting how tired you must be. Of course we must return straight away.'

He set the car in motion and when he made no attempt to speak, not even to discuss the project they'd just visited, Lily was left feeling that she had disappointed him in some way.

'I'll speak to him later,' she said aloud in the seclusion of her own private bathroom as the tepid water refreshed her sticky body. 'I'll tell him that I would have *loved* to go with him…' A giant yawn threatened to drown her and she gave a gurgle of laughter. 'Sleep, woman!' she ordered herself as she shut off the tap. 'Maybe your brain will work better then.'

Razak felt uncomfortably like a voyeur as he stood in the darkness outside Lily's room the following night.

He'd just wasted his time having another cold shower and had been about to try to catch up on some sleep when he'd realised he still hadn't told her about the door that led from her room out into the atrium. He should have told her yesterday, when he'd shown her to the room, but every logical thought had gone out of his head when he'd seen her smiling at the birds' aerial acrobatics.

The building was far too old and vast to make installing air-conditioning feasible so the family still relied on the centuries-old methods of circulating the air cooled by the shade of the colonnade and the nearby expanse of water by opening their doors and windows. As an experiment, they'd replaced some of the old pierced screens with gauzy curtains that not only preserved their privacy and helped to keep out flying insects but also allowed more light into the rooms.

He'd donned his robe and stepped out of his door to make the short journey along the colonnade to her room, but when he'd tapped on the glass there had been no answer.

All he'd intended had been to open the door enough to allow a cooling breeze to flow into her room but when the edge of the curtain had fluttered aside for a second he'd caught sight of her lying in the middle of the enormous bed and hadn't been able to look away.

In all the weeks he'd known her he'd never seen her with

her hair loose about her shoulders this way. He could only guess exactly how long it was and how soft it would feel between his fingers.

And her skin…

He clenched his hands tightly to try to dampen the tingling as he imagined touching and stroking and exploring to discover if it was as silky as it looked. The colour was almost unearthly in the moonlight reflected into the room by the water outside, with the ivory luminosity of the rarest of pearls. He could imagine all too easily what her skin would look like beside his, the colour combination very like her favourite *crème brûlée* dessert.

A sudden sound had his head whipping around to find his brother standing in his open doorway, watching.

Even as he stepped back from Lily's room he saw Karim begin to shake his head in a chiding way but with a devilish light in his eyes.

'What do you want?' Razak growled, as he stepped back into his own room, guilt making him abrupt.

'I am the bearer of news, both good and bad, big brother,' Karim said, with his hands held up defensively. 'Which order would you prefer them?'

There was something in Karim's eyes that made his stomach clench, but he'd never considered himself a coward.

'The bad news first,' he said, and braced himself. As long as his father wasn't any worse…

'You were seen in Lily's room yesterday morning.'

'Of course I was. I showed her to the room soon after we arrived and—'

'Kissing her,' Karim added pointedly, and Razak closed his eyes, grimly remembering the curtain he'd seen moving on the other side of the atrium. He'd been so distracted by her presence in his childhood home that he'd completely forgotten just how many pairs of eyes there were about the place.

'And?' He drew in a deep breath, knowing the worst was still to come.

'Mother-dear knows and is incandescent with rage against the foreigner who brings her blatant sinful ways to seduce you from your honour and your duty.'

Razak sighed heavily with the weight of unwanted responsibility. 'And yet there is good news, too?'

'Always, even in the darkest hour,' his brother reminded him softly. 'And this is the news that Father is progressing even better than expected since you came home. In fact, his surgeon is saying that it is possible he may be allowed home in a matter of days and definitely before the end of the week.'

'That *is* good news,' Razak said with a surge of relief and joy. As a doctor he knew how dreadful patients could look soon after surgery, but he'd been shocked by just how much weaker and older his father had suddenly seemed since the last time he'd seen him.

Seeing him lying helpless in that hospital bed hooked up to all those monitors had brought it home to him more forcefully than ever before that the man who had given him life would not survive for ever.

In the meantime…

In the meantime, there were decisions that had to be made, things that had been done many years ago that needed to be unravelled, no matter how angry it made his mother…

'Such deep thoughts,' Karim mocked gently.

'And so little time left in which to think them,' Razak countered. 'Have you thought any more about—?'

'I have thought about little else,' his brother interrupted hotly. 'I never dreamed that you would contemplate breaking an alliance of such long standing. Can you imagine the scandal?'

'It would be more scandalous if we were to go ahead, especially as we have always known that it is not what either of us wanted…and more especially so if *you* are now contemplating…shall we call it a substitution?'

'More than contemplating,' Karim said firmly, a new resolution to the angle of his head as he met his brother's gaze. 'If you are serious in your intention to revoke…?'

'I *am* serious,' Razak said, filled with sudden certainty. 'I know it will cause uproar, but hopefully you will be able to deflect that fairly swiftly with an announcement of your own. You are, after all, the politician in the family.'

'And?' Karim questioned with a tilt of his head in the direction of Lily's room through the adjoining wall.

'And…it is probably much too soon for her to know but, as far as I am concerned, there is no question.'

CHAPTER EIGHT

LILY pressed back against the ancient wall, hoping that she would be invisible in the deep shadows of the colonnade if anyone else ventured out.

She had no idea what had woken her—possibly the sound of Razak's voice through the open door that led out to the atrium, although she hadn't realised that it was open until she saw the filmy curtain billowing gently and had no memory of opening it.

Unable to resist listening to him speak, captivated as ever by the way his husky accent rippled over her nerves, it was several seconds before she realised that he wasn't using his own tongue but the English he and Karim had admitted to using when they wanted to be certain that their conversation couldn't be understood by the staff and passed on to their mother.

She had no idea what they were talking about. It could have been a business contract or some political alliance, but there was something odd about the intensity of their voices and the way they cut so quickly into each other's sentences that made her think that it was something far more personal.

Not that she would ever be able to ask because that would

mean admitting to eavesdropping just because she loved the sound of his voice.

And it wasn't just the sound of his voice that she loved—it was everything about the man, from his commitment to his work to his willingness to fight bureaucracy for a better deal for his patients to the conscientious way he made certain that she had plenty of opportunities to hone her own operating skills.

Then, of course, there was the way he looked so lean and powerful that she had to catch her breath every time she saw him, and when he looked at her with those dark eyes it was impossible to break their gaze.

'Talk about wishing for the moon,' she whispered wryly, knowing that someone as work-orientated and just plain ordinary as her would never stand a chance of attracting someone as devastating as Razak Khan. His mother certainly didn't think she belonged here with him but if she had even half a chance…

'Why him?' she breathed, closing her eyes tight against the threat of tears even as she felt the first seed of despair unfurling inside her. She'd barely noticed the other men she'd studied and worked with over the years. Why did she have to go and fall in love with someone so…so impossible, so unattainable?

She thought she'd managed to stifle the stupid sob that rose up in her throat but she must have made a sound because the next thing she knew he was there in front of her, a dark silhouette against the beaten silver of the moonlit pool behind him.

'Jasmine?' he murmured, framing her shoulders with the gentle warmth of his hands and angling his head to peer into her face. 'Is there something wrong? You are unwell? Unhappy?'

Unhappy? With his gentle hands on her and his voice filled with concern? With his warmth surrounding her, carrying with it the unique mixture of soap and pheromones that her receptors seemed to have been programmed to recognise?

Her body was receiving so much sensory input that she was about to go into meltdown.

'N-no,' she stammered uncertainly, wishing she knew how to put all her feelings into words, but she had so little experience with men and none at all with being in love.

He had begun to stroke the bare skin of her shoulders with soothing circles of his fingertips and she shivered in response.

'You are cold,' he said. 'You should go inside, away from the breeze.' But when she thought he would have ushered her into her room and returned to his own, he accompanied her through the gauzy curtains and turned her to face him again.

Nervously she raised her eyes to his, suddenly aware that her every expression would be visible in the soft light reflected in by the pool, that he would be able to tell how much the sight of his body, naked to the waist and so tantalisingly close to her own, was affecting her.

'Don't look away,' he whispered when she would have tried to hide her emotions from him. He cupped his supple surgeon's fingers around her face and tilted it up towards his again and she was lost, gazing into those dark eyes that had captivated her the first time she'd seen them and had drawn the snare tighter with every glance over the top of a disposable mask.

'Razak... I...' She paused uncertainly to flick the tip of her tongue over her lips, her mouth suddenly dry with nerves the instant that she'd decided to tell him what was in her heart.

Only she never had the chance to say those words.

She'd seen his eyes follow her tongue back into her mouth and with a sudden groan he was pressing his lips to hers and his tongue was exploring the warm welcoming depths.

This was very different from the almost chaste brush of his lips over hers the morning they'd arrived. This was so intense that it was almost frightening, except this was Razak, the man she'd fallen headlong in love with before she'd even realised that it had happened, and she could never be frightened of him.

'Jasmine,' he whispered, as he buried his face in the angle between throat and shoulder and again when he found the curve of her breast over the edge of the camisole top of the plain cotton nightdress she'd worn to go to sleep. Then his seeking hands explored its all too brief hem and discovered the skimpy briefs she'd worn for coolness and she nearly went up in flames.

'Razak!' she groaned helplessly, overwhelmed by the unexpected collision of sensation and emotion. She had no idea where any of this was going. All she knew was that she didn't want it to stop…ever.

'Touch me,' he demanded raggedly. 'If you want me as much as I want you, put your hands on me and… Ah-h, Jasmine!' he groaned when she took him at his word and placed both hands on his chest to discover for the first time what the whorls of dark hair that patterned its width felt like.

Something deep inside her had clenched tight at the realisation that he wanted this as much as she did and the fact that she had his permission to touch and explore sent a wave of delight through her.

'It's silky,' she whispered, as she ran her fingertips over

the dark swathe then tunnelled them through the thickness of it until she encountered hard male nipples.

He gave a sharp hiss when she dragged an experimental nail over each and she froze, worried that she might have hurt him, then she saw the almost feral gleam in those dark eyes and realised that it certainly wasn't pain he was feeling.

'My turn,' he decreed in a growl, and before she realised what he was going to do he'd grabbed the lower edge of her nightdress and drawn it over her head. 'Ah, Jasmine, no,' he said, catching her hands when she would have covered herself. 'Don't hide such perfection,' he whispered as he cupped each breast in the warmth of his hands. 'Look at the two of us together, my skin making yours look so pale and creamy. We are like your favourite *crème brûlée* come to life.'

She could see exactly what he meant, the deep natural tan of his body making hers seem even paler by comparison, especially where he was moulding the soft swell of her breasts with his clever fingers and… 'Oh,' she breathed on a sudden gasp of breath when he feathered his thumbs across them and her nipples furled into tight buds.

'So responsive,' he murmured, as he lowered his head and made her gasp again as he took first one and then the other into the heat of his mouth. The sensation was so overwhelming that her knees forgot how to hold her weight, but that was no problem when there were Razak's strong arms to scoop her up and carry her across to the bed.

He laid her down as carefully as though she were a fragile newborn and deliberately spread her hair out across the pillows before straightening up to look at her.

For a moment she wanted to squirm with embarrassment, knowing how lacking she was in all the things that men usually…

'Perfect,' he said, and stopped her thoughts in their well-worn tracks. 'I tried to imagine how you would look—dreamed of you, too—but…' He shook his head as his eyes roved over her from head to foot and back again. 'You are truly as beautiful as your name—a slender, elegant lily,' he said, and there was such sincerity in his voice that for the first time in her life she actually found herself believing it.

Then she saw his hands reach for the fastening at the waist of his trousers and all thoughts of her own shortcomings were forgotten in her anticipation of seeing his body completely naked for the first time.

She already knew that he was lean and muscular from the way his theatre scrubs fitted his body and that his legs were almost as darkly furred as the impressive patterns on his chest, but…

'Oh!' she exclaimed, and felt her eyes widen with a mixture of admiration and trepidation when he turned to face her and she saw the unmistakable evidence of his desire.

It wasn't as if she hadn't seen that particular part of the male anatomy before. She had, many times over the years of her medical training, but never one quite so…

'Ah, my Jazz, you are so good for my ego!' he said with a chuckle as he joined her on the bed and pulled her back into his arms, sending shivers up and down her spine when he nuzzled her throat and whispered huskily in her ear. 'And now that I know that the appearance didn't disappoint you, I will have to make certain that the performance doesn't either.'

His body seemed warmer than ever as he wrapped her in

his arms and she just had time to feel the way the silky pelt on his chest teased her sensitive nipples as he leant over her before his lips met hers again and she was opening her mouth eagerly to welcome the swift invasion of his tongue.

And when kissing alone wasn't enough, her hands set off on their own journey of exploration, tracing the curve of the back of his head and the strong column of his neck, fingers spreading wide to measure the width of his shoulders and sliding down the length of his back to the lean planes of his hips and the tight curves of his buttocks.

'No more,' he groaned, capturing one inquisitive hand and bringing it up to his mouth for a kiss.

Lily froze, wondering what on earth she had done wrong, but she didn't have long to wonder when he continued with an air almost of embarrassment.

'It has been a very long time for me, my sweet jasmine flower, and I have wanted you from the first day I met you. If you touch me any more I will not be able to control…to go slow enough to bring you the pleasure you deserve.'

She couldn't bear it. Her body had recognised its mate and couldn't wait a second longer for his possession.

'Razak, please…now!' she begged, and almost whimpered with relief when he finally positioned himself over her.

Even as he made that first connection, a tiny remnant of self-preservation was telling her that she should warn him of her innocence, but logic told her that this had gone too far for belated fears. She arched eagerly to welcome him and winced when he met the tell-tale barrier.

She hoped desperately that he hadn't noticed but in the blink of an eye he'd grown rigid in her arms and although she couldn't understand a single word she had a good idea what he was saying to her as he sprang off the bed and strode across to the window.

Suddenly embarrassed by her nudity, she pulled the corner of the bedspread over herself but her shivers didn't ease.

'Razak?' she said to his bowed back, conscious even in the midst of her disappointment of the hands braced on either side of the window, showcasing the breadth of his shoulders and the narrowness of his waist and hips.

What could she say? *I'm sorry I'm still a virgin?*

'Why?' he demanded tautly, without turning to face her, and she began to feel irritated by his attitude.

'What do you mean, *why?* Why am I still a virgin at my age or why didn't I tell you or—?'

'I was actually going for the more important ones,' he interrupted, finally turning to face her with one fist firmly planted on each hip so that she had to meet his turbulent gaze; she was suddenly far too embarrassed to allow her eyes to drop any lower. 'Why have you never wanted to do this before when you are such a passionate woman? Why me? Why now?'

Her anger disappeared in a flash when she realised that she couldn't give him the only answer he needed. In the heat of passion she'd nearly blurted it out but she just couldn't do it like this, huddled in the middle of the bed while he confronted her from the other side of the room.

There was one answer that made all the others irrelevant—that she'd fallen in love with him.

That was the reason why she'd never wanted to make love before...because she'd never been in love. And if she confessed that, there would be no need for the *Why me?* or *Why now?* questions.

Somewhere in the back of her brain a quotation surfaced from a long-ago history lesson—*The best method of defence is attack*—and she realised that was now her only option.

'Whereas for you, an obviously passionate man, the question is why did you stop? Were you afraid I wouldn't know enough to satisfy you, or perhaps you were afraid I'd expect you to marry me if you destroyed the proof of my innocence?'

The next day Lily's luck finally ran out.

Well, she really had no idea whether it had been luck that had kept her out of contact with Razak's disapproving mother or whether he'd been cleverly making certain that the two of them were never in the same place at the same time. Perhaps it was just that she hadn't been able to sleep a wink last night for replaying every delicious caress only to cringe as she'd remembered the insulting speed with which Razak had leapt from the bed as soon as he'd realised that he'd nearly become her first.

Obviously Razak hadn't changed his mind about anything overnight because this morning it was almost as if he'd completely disappeared.

She'd waited with her stomach full of nervous knots but he hadn't knocked on her door to escort her to breakfast. Finally, even though she wasn't convinced that she'd be able to eat a thing, she refused to cower in her room any longer and set off on her own.

When she really didn't care one way or the other, she found the room without a single wrong turn. Unfortunately, the only person there to applaud her achievement was Razak's mother, and by the time Lily realised that she was the person sitting in the beautiful breakfast salon it was too late to retreat, even though the last thing she needed that morning was another confrontation.

Her elegant silk suit was perfect enough to be a designer original and Lily guessed that it probably cost more than a month's salary and there wasn't a hair out of place on her elegantly coiffed head, but there was a less genuine welcome on her face than if she'd been a tailor's dummy.

'Good morning,' Lily said brightly, as she firmly rejected the option of turning on her heel and scuttling back to safety. 'I hope you don't mind if I join you?'

In the absence of anything more than a tight-lipped stare for a reply, she turned to pour herself a cup of aromatic coffee, proud that her hands were perfectly steady. With a croissant and a couple of fresh figs on a plate, she chose a seat almost at the other end of the table and wondered if she would choke herself to death with her first mouthful.

'Do you know if Razak has already left to visit his father?' Lily asked, as she split the flaky pastry and reached for the dish of butter. She'd thought it a sufficiently innocuous topic of conversation, but obviously just the mention of her son's name was enough to release the torrent of words the woman had been holding back since the moment Lily had set foot in the house.

'You are wasting your time, chasing after my son,' she said precisely and almost without expression. 'You have been blatant with your sinful ways. You have been trying to seduce Razak from his duties but it will not work. My son is the first-born and he is an honourable man who will not turn from the path he has been destined to tread.'

It wasn't just that her accent was far stronger than those of the other members of their family that made it difficult for Lily to understand what she was saying. What she did know was that the woman was seriously disturbed by her presence in Razak's life. Well, after last night she had absolutely nothing to worry about, but Lily could hardly tell her that.

'Your son and I are colleagues at work,' she began calmly, deliberately suppressing the pain it caused to know that after the dreadful final seconds in her room last night, colleagues were all they would ever be. 'He is teaching me all about the new operating method he's setting up at my hospital so that when his contract ends and he comes to work at the hospital here—'

'Do not think that you can fool me!' the older woman interrupted heatedly, her cheeks darkening as her control slipped a notch. 'We have all seen the way you look at him and lure him into your rooms like a common…'

Lily didn't need to understand the language to know that she'd been insulted, but before she could find polite words of her own to object, the imperious woman was speaking again.

'Anyway, this doctoring, it does not matter!' his mother snapped with a dismissive gesture of a heavily beringed hand. 'It is not Razak's destiny to cut bodies up like the man who slaughters animals for the kitchen. As the first-born son it is his destiny to follow his father, to take his rightful place as leader of—'

'Of course being a surgeon matters to Razak,' she argued swiftly, not caring how rude it was to interrupt her elder. Denigrating their profession as nothing more than butchery was one thing, but to suggest that Razak would be willing to abandon it any time soon to take over as a mere figurehead of some business corporation was nonsense. 'He has worked hard for many years to perfect his skill and is one of the most gifted men I've ever seen or worked with. You're fooling yourself if you think he'd ever give it up.'

There was deep anger in the woman's eyes when she stared Lily down and for a second she almost believed the woman capable of doing her physical violence. Then she saw a calculating edge creep into her expression and knew that she had a trump card to play.

'You do not know my son as well as you think you do,' she said coldly, each word coated with its own measure of venom. 'He will give medicine up as easily as he will toss you out where you belong because he knows it is his duty.'

She deposited her linen napkin beside her plate and rose elegantly to her feet, somehow seeming far taller in her scorn.

'As soon as he has fulfilled his contract in England, he will take the place that has been destined to be his since the minute he was born and he will marry the woman who has been intended to be his wife ever since they were betrothed.'

'Betrothed?' Lily hadn't even realised that she'd echoed the word until she saw the victorious sneer on the woman's face.

'Oh, dear. Didn't he tell you about Dita?' she asked with a cloying pretence at solicitousness. 'She is such a beautiful girl, the perfect one to be his wife. His father chose her for him many years ago from the family of one of his closest friends and allies, and if you know anything at all about Razak you will know that he is an honourable man who would never go against his father's wishes.'

Lily was left listening to the sharp click of the woman's Italian leather court shoes as she walked swiftly out of the room, and all she could hope was that the shock of that revelation had kept her expression so frozen that Razak's mother would never know the depth of the devastation she had left in her wake.

CHAPTER NINE

RAZAK was getting married?

There was a strange roaring sound in Lily's ears as the words echoed over and over in her head and her nails were making deep indentations in the perfect damask tablecloth as she concentrated on staying upright in her seat.

Razak's whole team had always known that as soon as his contract ended he was coming back to work in his own country. The detail he'd forgotten to tell anyone was the fact that he already had a fiancée waiting in the wings ready for him to come home.

So what had last night been about? A convenient fling with a warm, willing body?

They had both known that it would be inappropriate for him to have made any advances while they had been at work in England, not least because he was her mentor. Hospitals had strict rules specifically to prevent sexual harassment of junior staff by their seniors.

Ah, but did those rules still apply when those two members of staff were thousands of miles away in a different country altogether, and when neither of them was even remotely on duty?

Or were they?

Razak had specifically said that the two of them were going to be working on the fine details of the new operating procedures while they were away. Did that mean that they were still officially working and that…?

'Oh, for heaven's sake! What's the point?' she muttered fiercely under her breath as she pushed away her untouched croissant and the tepid cup of coffee. The invisible staff that kept this enormous place running like a well-oiled piece of machinery were probably waiting just out of sight to clear the table of the breakfast debris and give it another coat of polish.

She, on the other hand, had no particular place to go and nothing to do except take stock of what a monumental fool she'd made of herself, and the only sane place to do that with so many eyes around was behind a locked door.

To her immense relief, one of the invisible army had been to her room while she'd been pretending to have breakfast. The bed had been freshly made and everything returned to pristine tidiness so there wasn't a single visible reminder of what had so nearly happened in there.

Still, she couldn't face sitting in the bedroom any more than she'd been able to make herself use the bed last night. Neither after those lonely hours of darkness, could she face sitting another moment on the elegant sofa where she might catch a glimpse of another of those captivating birds out by the pool.

The bathroom was as neutral as it got and had a couple of added advantages—first, that it had no windows, so any sound she made in there wouldn't be heard by anyone passing by and, second, there was a wide expanse of mirrors along one wall so she could take a good long look at herself while she got her head together.

The first thing she knew without needing any debate was that she wouldn't be making any sort of harassment accusation against Razak.

How could she? She'd been every bit as eager for it to happen as he had. It was actually a point in his favour that he'd been able to call a halt when he had, because she certainly hadn't wanted to.

Well, it wouldn't be happening again, not now she knew about…whatever-her-name…*Dita*. That was it. The perfect, hand-picked, high-octane bride, and so much more appropriate for Mr Razak Khan, Consultant Orthopaedic Surgeon, than his junior, Dr Lily Nobody.

Well, the woman might be his perfect wife, but she certainly wasn't his perfect second pair of hands in the operating theatre. Dita wasn't the one who was going to be working with him for the rest of his contract, spending every second learning everything she could from him until she'd sucked him dry of everything he had to give.

And by the time he left, there wouldn't be a hospital in the country…in the whole civilised world…that wouldn't be beating her door down to have her on their staff. And by the time she finally made consultant, she would never even think about the first man she'd ever fallen in love with or his starkly beautiful country and especially not all his wonderful plans for the future that she would never be a part of.

She certainly wouldn't let anything like this happen again…she wouldn't be able to, because she didn't have a heart left now that Razak had stolen it and destroyed it.

'Hey, Dr Langley! When did you get back?' Chloe Westerham called as soon as she spotted Lily coming into the ward. It wasn't yet time for rounds but she hadn't been able to wait to see how the brave young woman was doing after her operation. 'What was it like? I bet you had a fabulous time. Was it all camels and palm trees or what?'

'Not a single camel as far as I can remember,' Lily said. 'But, then, we were in the capital city, so I suppose that's a bit like a visitor here expecting to see a Dartmoor pony or the monarch of the glen in London.'

Chloe giggled at the idea but Lily could hear a definite edge to it, as though she was trying just a bit too hard. Was her own misery making her more sensitive to her patient's woes or was she projecting her own feelings onto her completely erroneously?

'How has it been going, Chloe?' she asked, as she quickly glanced through the record of what had been happening in their absence, deliberately settling herself on the edge of the bed as though she had plenty of time for a chat. 'Your file looks good… No infections…in fact, no post-op problems of any kind. You're obviously the perfect patient.'

'That's me. Just perfect,' Chloe agreed, but this time there was a quiver to her lower lip and a quaver to her voice and the skin around her eyes was suspiciously blotchy as though she'd been doing some serious crying in the recent past.

'Chloe?' Lily prompted gently, needing to know what was worrying the young woman if she was going to be able to do anything to help.

'*So* perfect, in fact,' Chloe continued, tipping her chin up in a show of bravado totally at odds with the glitter of tears already gathering, 'that my best friend Shayna came in yesterday morning to ask me *not* to be her bridesmaid after all because she doesn't want me ruining the video of their happy day by clomping up the aisle behind her on my tin leg, still looking as if I've had my head shaved.'

'Oh, sweetheart,' Lily murmured, knowing how much her patient had been through and how much she'd been looking forward to taking part in the ceremony. It had actually been an important motivator, making her all the more determined to work hard at her months of arduous rehab specifically so that she *wouldn't* be doing dot-and-carry-one as she carried her friend's train. And, anyway, her hair was already regrowing since the chemo had stopped.

'And then, yesterday evening, just to make my day even more perfect, my boyfriend—you know, the one I've been going out with since for ever and who's been proposing once a week ever since Shayna and Billy started planning their wedding—well, he came to visit me to say that he wouldn't be going out with me any more. He doesn't mind the hair because he knows that'll grow back eventually, but the idea that I've had cancer and had to have one of my bones replaced with metal completely freaks him out and he can't b-bear to be near me any m-more…'

Murmuring wordless comfort, Lily whisked the curtain around the bed to give them an illusion of privacy then gathered the sobbing girl into her arms, cradling and rocking her as if she were a baby until the tears finally dwindled.

'I'm *so* sorry, Doctor,' Chloe sniffed, clearly mortified that she'd broken down like that, and in front of one of the medical staff.

'Hey, none of that, Chloe! You aren't the first to need a cry and you definitely won't be the last.' Lily leaned forward and beckoned her closer, immediately capturing the seventeen-year-old's attention before she whispered, 'I vaguely remember that there's a special rule about this sort of situation. It's something that says when a patient cries all over you, they're entitled to call you by your first name whenever there aren't any other members of staff around. Had you heard about that rule?'

'Not till today,' Chloe said with a watery smile.

'Well, we can't possibly break the rules,' Lily said sternly, refusing to think about the rules she'd broken with Razak even if he'd stopped short of the final one. 'So, from now on I'm Lily.'

'Lily? Well, we didn't guess *that* one,' Chloe said with a hint of a smile. 'We were playing a game…us patients… trying to guess the first names of the staff who'd only put their initials on their badges. We went through all the L names we could think of but none of us came up with Lily.'

Lily pulled a face. 'It's a family thing. All the females are named after flowers—Rose, Iris and so on—and when I put on a spurt of growth when I was about thirteen, one of my sisters suggested renaming me dandelion because I was growing like a weed.'

The laughter was more genuine this time, but it didn't last long, the memories of the double blow she'd received the previous day still weighing heavily on Chloe's mind.

'I was so looking forward to being a bridesmaid,' she said in a very small voice, tears beginning to well again. 'And as Shayna's always been my best friend, it was going to be the only chance I had to do it. And now I'm not even going to be able to look forward to going up the aisle on my *own* wedding day.'

Lily had barely begun to weave those sorts of fantasies around her relationship with Razak, but the knowledge that she'd already lost the only man she'd ever wanted meant that she knew how the young woman was feeling.

'Well, Chloe, I don't know if it's much consolation at the moment, but if I ever get married, I want you to promise that you'll be my bridesmaid…even if it takes till I'm 90 and in a wheelchair.'

'You're on!' the pretty teenager exclaimed a little soggily, shaking the hand that Lily had offered to seal the pact. 'I shall usher you up the aisle on my Zimmer frame and in return you have to promise that you'll throw your bouquet straight at me to make sure I can catch it.'

Something caught her eye over Lily's shoulder and it was her turn to beckon her closer to whisper, 'Hey, Lily, we didn't manage to guess Mr Khan's name either. He's far too exotic-looking for it to be Roger or Richard. Any clues?'

It took Lily a second or two to get her brain working once she knew that Razak was somewhere close behind her, but the new, tougher version of Dr Lily Langley could achieve anything she set her mind to.

'Oh, I couldn't possibly say,' she said with a cheerful smile as she stood up, ready to make her escape as soon as her nemesis was busy with another patient. 'That would be cheating.'

Lily was still avoiding him, Razak realised when he looked up a moment later and she was nowhere in sight.

She'd grown all too adept at that little trick in their final two days in his home so that he'd initially been delighted when his mother had insisted on organising an elaborate meal to welcome his father home from the hospital.

He'd hoped that being forced into each other's company

like that would have helped to ease the atmosphere between the two of them, but to his mother's obvious delight it had only become worse with every attempt he'd made to talk to her.

In the end, the return flight that he'd been pinning so many hopes on had been a complete disaster as she'd refused to say a single word or listen to anything he had to say, apparently escaping almost immediately into sleep and only waking up in time to grab her bag, disembark and hail a taxi to take her home.

Well, she couldn't avoid him for ever, especially with the ceremony to mark the opening of the new theatre suite taking place that evening and their first batch of patients being admitted tomorrow afternoon for surgery the following morning.

Even so, nothing seemed to stop his level of frustration from rising, especially when he was certain that all she needed to do was listen for a few minutes to his explanation and they could go on from there.

He'd been so amazed—and strangely, primitively triumphant—to discover that she'd never made love before that it had taken him some time to realise that Lily had taken his withdrawal as outright rejection. All he needed was enough uninterrupted time with her to explain why he'd felt that her innocence shouldn't be squandered like that but should be treated as the special gift it was.

'Hah! Chance would be a fine thing!' he muttered aloud as he strode along the corridor, making one of the cleaners take a hasty step back into the storeroom with his trolley full of mops and buckets.

He'd been so keyed up with everything that was going on in his life that he'd arrived for work hours before his shift had been due to start that morning and had ploughed doggedly through the mountain of accumulated paperwork that had been waiting for his attention, longing for the moment when Lily would arrive and he could fill his eyes with her slender perfection.

But the more he tried to engineer such a meeting, the more he began to suspect that there was something more…something deeper that had taken the sparkle out of those beautiful eyes when she looked in his direction now.

Well, he would just have to compose his soul in patience and take his opportunities where he could find them, starting with the little bit of pomp and circumstance to celebrate the completion of the new facility that evening.

'I don't really have an option,' he said flatly, his heart clenching when he contemplated a future without Lily in it. He didn't know how it had happened, but she now meant so much to him that it felt as if it would be easier to live without breathing than to lose his precious jasmine flower.

Five minutes into the rather pointless ceremony, he realised that Lily was every bit as determined to stay away from him as he was to be close to her. When Reg glared at him for the second time for paying less than complete attention to the obliging member of the minor nobility who was to cut the scarlet ribbon, he pinned his hopes instead on the departmental meal he had suggested at a popular restaurant.

Even there, Lily had outmanoeuvred him by volunteering to stand in at the hospital so that other members of the team would be free to attend. Razak was left with an aching face from having to work so hard to look as if he was enjoying himself and an aching heart from the depressing thought that he might have done irreparable damage to their fledgling relationship.

The one place that Lily would never be able to avoid him was when the two of them were in Theatre, and the first session with the two rooms being used simultaneously got off to a flying start with every single member of their elite team turning up early.

'It is good that you are all so enthusiastic,' Razak said, with a smile to camouflage his own first-day jitters. Admissions had gone as smooth as silk yesterday afternoon with every single patient turning up at the appointed time and testing fit for surgery.

'It's great that we're finally going to be given the chance to see this system in operation…if you'll excuse the pun,' Tim said, rubbing his hands in anticipation of a busy morning's work.

'Is everybody satisfied that we have enough supplies to last the morning, or at least that we'll be able to restock without any delays?'

'Everything's been double-checked,' the theatre manager confirmed. 'We'll be ready for the first patient to come into Theatre A by seven-twenty to be prepped for surgery, and you should be starting your bit of the job by eight.'

'So, as the first case is relatively straightforward…' He'd deliberately scheduled a day of the less problematic patients so that everyone could get used to the new system with as little stress as possible. 'We'll probably need the second patient in Theatre B at about eight-twenty as I should be finished in here by nine.'

At least, that was the plan, and while his hand-picked team were all eager to prove that it was a far better way of utilising the hospital's resources, there were at least an equal number of people anticipating the chance to crow when the new system collapsed in chaos.

Well, it would be *his* fault if that happened. He would only have himself to blame for not doing the groundwork properly…that, and the fact that he could hardly keep his mind on the job when he was trying to catch a glimpse of Lily before they started.

'Concentrate,' he muttered softly inside his mask an hour later, even as his eyes lingered on the shadows darkening the fine skin beneath her eyes. Was it nerves about the operations today that had robbed her of her sleep or had she been thinking about him…about the fact that they would sometimes be every bit as close as they'd been on her bed when he'd so nearly…

Her pupils widened as he held her gaze for several long seconds and he suddenly wondered just how much of his thoughts she could read.

Suddenly embarrassed that he might be metaphorically wearing his heart on his sleeve—or at least a goodly proportion of his hormones—he dragged his eyes down to the open incision in front of him.

'Suction,' he said, but the word had barely left his mouth and she was already clearing the operating field as though she'd known exactly what he was going to need. He permitted himself one final thought that it was a pity she wasn't so willing to accommodate his other pressing need…for conversation, if nothing else.

Well, if the only way she would let him be close to her was in the operating theatre, then he hoped she was prepared to work harder than she ever had in her life, because for the life of his contract he was going to pour all his energies into helping her to be the best surgeon she could possibly be. Perhaps that would be the way back into her heart.

A month later the only thing Razak could be certain of was that his belief in Lily's surgical skills had been well placed.

She'd risen to every challenge he'd thrown in her path and mastered it, and he couldn't be more delighted...well, that was a lie, but the chance of her delighting him by agreeing to a private conversation seemed as remote as ever.

He looked out of his office window at the patch of blue sky that had been widening all morning and suddenly felt the need to get out of the hospital. He was due for a few hours off duty and the chance to take stock of how far he'd come.

Even in his wildest dreams he hadn't imagined that the new system would go so smoothly, and while there had been some initial grumbles from the nurses in the post-op and surgical wards about their increased workload, that had quickly faded as they'd discovered a new enthusiasm for their work. With his waiting list shrinking by the week, it was amazing what a difference it made to have patients who weren't bitter about the length of time they'd had to wait and this had rubbed off on the nurses taking care of them.

He was certain it also had an effect on the patients' recovery time, with the latest batch all doing well, some of the minor cases already at home with instructions to return for sutures to be removed.

The sign for the town he was entering read 'Ditchling' and rang a bell in his mind. One of his earliest personal referrals had been from the GP there and in his more desperate sleep-less hours he'd actually wondered whether he might stand a better chance with Lily if he applied to extend his contract and contacted all the practices in the towns around the hospital to build up the referral side of his work. Even when he'd completely got rid of his waiting lists there would always be some patients who wanted to go private for their surgery, and a personal contact with the GPs would hopefully put him to the forefront of their minds if they were asked for the name of a surgeon.

Before he had time to change his mind, there in front of him was the neat building that housed Ditchling's health centre and he pulled into an empty parking slot.

'So, I will go in and introduce myself,' he said aloud, in the confines of the car, hoping he wouldn't seem too much like a cold-calling salesman to Dr Willmott.

'Mr Khan,' the GP said with a smile as she entered the reception area. He straightened up from his inspection of the toys in the children's corner and as he returned her smile with one of his own he was able to put aside his fear that she would resent his unexpected visit.

'Please, if it would not offend you, you could call me Razak,' he invited, liking this softly spoken woman at once.

'And I'm Kat,' she responded, offering him her hand, and he marvelled that he felt not a tremor at the contact with her soft skin, so unlike his reaction to even the slightest contact with Lily.

'Cat, like the animal?' he enquired with a blink of surprise.

'No.' She chuckled. 'Kat, short for Katriona. Would you like to take a seat? I'm sure Rose wouldn't mind making us some coffee.'

He grinned at the motherly Rose, who had spent the entire time he'd been waiting for Kat to appear grilling him about himself. If he didn't miss his guess, that was definitely a matchmaking gleam in her eye.

'No coffee, thank you. I was driving in this direction, exploring your beautiful country, and decided to call into your surgery when I recognised the address. I don't want to take up too much of your time,' he added easily. 'Your Rose has already told me how busy you are with your son in hospital. It is good news that his operation has gone well.'

'The best,' Kat agreed wholeheartedly. 'Unless you've gone through something like that, knowing that there's a danger that your child is going to be seriously disabled by an operation but that if he *doesn't* have the surgery he'll probably die…' She shook her head wordlessly, and although Razak hoped he would never know such torment personally, he had seen it all too often and could empathise with her.

'My patients aren't usually in that life-or-death situation,' he admitted self-deprecatingly. 'Mostly, they are just pleased to be out of pain at last, those who have replacement joints, like your Mr Aldarini.'

'I did wonder if he was why you were here. Has there been a problem that you needed to come here in person?'

'No problem at all,' he reassured her. 'Mr Aldarini is only partly why I am here. He is recovering well, in spite of the fact he delayed having the operation for far too long. Mostly, I wanted to tell you that, with the tandem system trial at the hospital, we are managing to do many more operations than before, but I will only be here for a few more months before I return to my own country to set up a whole new department.

So I will need all the practice I can get and I wanted to let you know that if you have any more patients who are in a similar position or whose operations have been delayed unnecessarily, I would be willing for you to refer them to me directly.'

He saw her blink in surprise at the suggestion, knowing that the old system at the hospital called for patients to be referred to the department with little or no input as to which of the orthopaedic surgeons would eventually do the operation—hopefully, the one with the shortest list.

As a result of the publicity in the paper when the new theatre suite had been opened, she had actually contacted his receptionist directly, probably in the hope that he hadn't already inherited an enormous back list of people waiting impatiently for their operations to take place.

'Won't your superiors have something to say about that?' she queried warily, no doubt conscious that she was going to have to continue to deal with the orthopaedic department long after he had returned to his own country. He could appreciate that she couldn't afford to put anyone's nose out of joint.

'It will not be a problem,' he reassured her easily. 'They still work in their old way and have more patients waiting than they can manage, with waiting lists that stretch…' He demonstrated with his arms spread, almost like a fisherman describing the one that had got away.

He left not long after to make his leisurely way back to the hospital, pleased that he'd called on her. She was an intelligent, sympathetic GP and now that he'd explained his aims, he was guessing that she was probably already planning to go through her patient list to find the names of those who would benefit from an operation sooner rather than later.

'And if she spreads the word…' he murmured as he waited at a set of lights, eager to be on his way again, then laughed at what he was saying. 'Fool! The hospital's already got more patients on its lists than it can cope with. At least give the new system a few more weeks to whittle away at the numbers before you start inviting more for their initial consultation.'

Still, there was definitely a feeling of satisfaction that it wouldn't be long before he could offer them a date for their surgery that wasn't an insult to their level of pain and disability and it was one that Kat had clearly shared.

She was a nice lady, he pondered as he set off again, and there had been the same idle appreciation for a good-looking member of the opposite sex in her eyes as she'd met him, but it had been easy to tell that there hadn't been a single spark in either direction.

Unlike the first time he'd met Lily when every nerve ending in his body had seemed to fire simultaneously, brought to life by nothing more than a pair of blue-grey eyes and that indefinable something that had never happened to him before.

Suddenly a leisurely trip back wasn't nearly fast enough and he found himself pressing just a little harder on the accelerator, anxious to get back to the hospital just so that he could be closer to Lily.

Lily held her breath and counted to ten as Razak shouldered his way through the doors, then blew the breath out slowly and deliberately behind her mask.

It was a stupid ritual, but concentrating on it was the only thing she'd found that could help her to control her body's instant reaction to his presence.

When was it ever going to start fading?

It had been many weeks since their trip to visit Razak's father and it seemed as strong as ever. The only thing she could say was that she'd learned the hard way how to focus on what needed to be done. She'd had to, because the only other alternative would have been to hand in her resignation, and that definitely hadn't been an option. It had taken her too many years and too much sacrifice to get this far, and with the many hours of experience she'd gained since they'd started the dual-theatre system, her surgical skills had improved exponentially.

Honesty made her admit that her rapid progress had been due in large part to Razak's unselfish tutoring. It was almost as if he'd read her mind and discovered her intention to absorb everything she could from him before he left, because he seemed to be equally intent on helping her every step of the way.

Today was a prime example of what he'd been doing, with the most interesting, unusual or complex case of the day reserved for last so that he could treat it like a teaching session. In the early days she'd done little more than watch and provide a second pair of hands when necessary, but as the weeks had gone on he'd entrusted her with more and more, and always with that sexy husky voice murmuring instruction, encouragement and praise.

He was so good at his job and so unendingly generous towards her that it made it difficult to find even a shred of lingering anger inside her. In fact, if anything, her love had just kept right on growing, in spite of the fact that she knew there was no possibility that it would ever be returned.

In the quiet misery of the night, she'd sometimes even thought that it might be worth trying to change his mind about going to bed with her just one time. At least then she would have the memory of a night spent in the arms of the man she loved to carry with her for the rest of her life.

The idea never got past the impossible daydream stage. All she had to do was remember the way he'd rejected her to know that he wouldn't be changing his mind about her any time soon, even though those dark, dark eyes still followed her every move with something in their depths that made her shiver in response.

'That's looking good, Jazz,' he said quietly, still stubbornly using the nickname he'd given her in spite of the fact that the first day she'd returned to the hospital after their trip she'd taken her music away and completely stopped using all her jasmine toiletries. She knew he'd noticed because he'd nearly broken her heart all over again on her birthday when he'd given her an exquisite cut-glass bottle of the most perfect jasmine essence she'd ever worn.

And she had worn it, just once. She hadn't been able to resist. But when the perfume had surrounded her and brought back all the happier moments between them, she'd had to scrub it off and had known she wouldn't be wearing it again.

But even though she'd stood for ages under a hot shower and had used copious quantities of soap to eradicate the last trace of it, the next time she met Razak's eyes it was as if he had known that she'd worn his gift on her skin, as if he had known every one of the pulse points she'd anointed with it and imagined tracing them with his lips the way he had that night…the inner curve of her elbows, over the frantically beating carotid pulse in her throat, between her breasts…

'Ready to re-articulate that joint?' he prompted, and she flicked the switch inside her head that brought her steely concentration back to the fore.

Silently, she positioned the new ball joint against the relined socket in exactly the way he'd shown her and with the minimum of effort it clicked straight into position, completely giving the lie to those like Reg who still thought orthopaedic surgery wasn't a suitable choice of specialty for women because they didn't have enough upper-body strength.

'Technique rather than power, yes?' Razak said, and she shivered at the uncanny way he always seemed to be able to tap into her thoughts.

His husky voice continued to stroke over her nerves. 'One of the surgeons I worked with in America had to stand on a step-up to reach the table properly and weighed so little that she probably had to run around under a shower to get wet, but she was a brilliant surgeon.' And when she heard the admiration in his voice Lily instantly hated the woman, hated any woman who could put a smile on his face when she couldn't.

But his admiration for that past colleague also fired her determination that one day he would say to one of his colleagues, *There was this surgeon I worked with in England...* The only trouble was, she wouldn't be there to hear it.

CHAPTER TEN

'YOU'VE got to go, Lily,' Tim said firmly.

Before she could even voice the belligerent 'Why' that rushed to her lips he was spelling out what she already knew.

'You *know* what this place is like for gossip,' he said wryly. 'And you've been working with the man for months. How could you not accept his invitation when the rest of us are all going, especially when the trip's all expenses paid?'

Lily wanted to cry that there was no amount of money and no threat of gossip that would make her travel back to the place where her heart had been so comprehensively broken, but then a fatalistic little voice in the back of her head joined in the persuasion.

You've got to go there, it said. *You've got to see it happen with your own eyes or you'll never be able to draw a line under it and get on with your life.*

The trouble was, she knew that Tim and the little voice were both right. She'd been hiding her head in the sand over the recent weeks and months, deliberately ignoring the fact that with each patient treated and each new skill mastered, her precious time with Razak was slipping past, that the day was drawing near when he would be gone from her life for ever.

The team had been working to capacity for several months now. With two theatres in use simultaneously, they'd easily managed to cope with two or three major operations and four or five minor ones in a single five-hour session.

The first time they'd actually managed to do six joint replacements in that time they'd all come out of Theatre on an adrenaline high.

It was going to be deadly dull if she had to go back to the time-wasting pedestrian pace of the other surgeons in the department…not that she knew that was what was going to happen because she hadn't even heard a whisper about Razak's replacement being appointed.

All she did know was that time was running out, and to add to that heartache was the invitation Razak had extended to the whole of his team to join him for an all-expenses-paid trip at the end of his contract to visit the new department he would be heading on his return home.

'Lily?' Tim said, and his tone told her it wasn't the first time he'd tried to attract her attention.

'Sorry Tim. I must have been wool-gathering,' she apologised, resigned to the fact that there really was no way she was going to be able to get out of it.

'I was just wondering why you never said anything about Razak's family when you came back last time,' he said, voicing a comment several had made when they'd discovered just which family Razak was related to. 'It can't be every day that you stay in a palace and talk to royalty.'

'Tim, I must be particularly dim, but I never even realised they were so important.' She shrugged, hoping no one would ever guess how astounded she'd been when she'd realised the truth. She could hardly believe that she'd actually contemplated having an affair with a man so far above her own humble origins. The Razak she knew and loved was a superbly skilled orthopaedic surgeon, not an all-important heir of an ancient dynasty. 'Ok, the house seemed big and old and sprawling and had some beautiful things in it,' she conceded, when Tim threw her an exasperated look, 'but I was more interested in visiting the new orthopaedic centre and finding out about Razak's plans for the running of it.'

Tim rolled his eyes. 'Well, this time you'll have to take more notice because we've been specially invited to the formal opening ceremony of the new department, followed by a private family celebration. We've all been warned to bring our best bib and tucker with us for that one.'

And Lily hadn't needed a reminder. She could still hear Razak's mother's delight when she'd informed the English nobody that Razak would be marrying his perfect bride as soon as he returned home. Every time she thought about witnessing the moment when she lost him for ever the pain tightened around her heart a little more, but she didn't really have any other option than to be there.

'You're right, Tim,' she said on a resigned sigh. 'We've all worked our cotton socks off for the man and helped him to prove that this system is the best cure for ludicrously long waiting lists. It's extraordinarily generous of him to invite us all to visit him for a week, and I promise that I shall go looking for something smart to wear so I don't let the department down.'

She managed to throw him a smile that finally wiped the worried frown off his face, though he seemed to understand just how much she wanted to refuse to go. There really wasn't any way that she could, not when she was going to have to work with all these people when they returned.

Tim was apparently more perceptive than most about the atmosphere between Razak and herself, but she was certain that no one other than the two of them knew about their near-miss all those months ago. There had been no gossip about the two of them so far, and that was the way she wanted it to stay.

'Oh, wow! Look at this place!' whispered Fliss Timmins, the circulating nurse in Theatre A, as she gazed around at the marble entrance hall. 'You could fit both our new theatres in here with room to spare.'

'I can't wait to see what the rest of it's like,' said one of the scrub nurses, her eyes equally wide. 'This is worth every extra minute I've spent on my feet since the new suite opened.'

'Welcome, everyone!' Razak said as he appeared at the other end of the room, closely followed by a whole phalanx of uniformed staff. He'd travelled out a day earlier than the rest of them to make certain that all the arrangements were in place and the busy hospital had felt strangely empty to Lily, knowing he would never work there again.

Geoff had the consultancy he'd been aiming for and had learned, just before he'd left for the airport, that he'd been appointed to take over Razak's position with the dual theatre system made a permanent part of the orthopaedic department. He'd joked that it had probably been Reg's idea in the hope that he was too inexperienced to maintain it and that it would swiftly collapse in chaos.

Lily had known that wasn't even a possibility. Razak had put too much of himself into setting the trial up and training the two of them for Geoff not to be able to cope with the challenging work, but she wasn't going to think about that now.

For the next week she was going to forget all about work. It was time to concentrate on consigning Razak to her past.

'I'm trying to be terribly well organised,' Razak announced to a ripple of laughter, his husky voice immediately drawing her attention, 'so when I call your name out—in strict alphabetical order, of course—will you each follow your guide, who will take you to your room. There will be an informal meal in just over an hour and then I've arranged to ferry all of us over to the hospital so you can have a good look at my new department before the dedication ceremony. Please, be aware that I would be completely delighted if every one of you decided to stay and work with me…'

They were all still chuckling as he began to read out their names one by one.

Lily had positioned herself towards the back of the group, taking advantage of the number of bodies between them to take in her fill of the handsome dark-eyed man laughing and teasing with his former colleagues.

She'd been afraid during the flight that she might not be able to keep her emotions under control when she saw him in his own home again, but she was just so glad to see him at all that she was coping. In fact, she would probably be quite all right just as long as he didn't single her out for any special treatment.

'Lily, would you go with Faria?' he called, with nothing more than a quick glance in her direction as a beautiful smiling young woman beckoned to her to follow her along the first of several long corridors.

Part of her was relieved that they were going in a different direction from her last stay here, while another was depressed that this time she wouldn't be staying anywhere near Razak. Then Faria opened the door on an even more luxurious suite than the last one she'd been given.

'Oh!' Lily exclaimed, when she saw the sumptuous hangings surrounding the bed and the priceless carpet spreading out in front of her feet. 'This is so beautiful. Are you sure it's for me?' she said, turning to question her guide, only to find that she'd disappeared, the door already closed silently behind her.

Lily couldn't resist exploring her temporary domain, marvelling over the totally modern bathroom with a walk-in shower spacious enough for half a dozen bodies at once and a bath nearly big enough to swim in.

It wasn't until she bounced on the bed to test the mattress that she realised just how vast the bed was and the fact that the beautiful silky hangings around the bed were there for more than decoration.

'What fun.' She giggled as she experimentally drew them together along one side of the bed, picturing how cosy it would feel to have the whole bed secluded in such a way if you were sharing it with…

'Dammit, don't go there!' she commanded herself aloud, as loss crashed over her again. In a matter of days…hours, even…Razak would be married to his Dita. It just felt wrong for her to imagine sharing this bed with him when he could never be hers.

There was a gentle tap at the door and her invitation brought the same dark-eyed beauty to lead her to the dining room to join the others.

'Heavens! I haven't unpacked my bag,' she exclaimed in a panic. She glanced round but couldn't see a sign of it. 'Well, it's too late to change into something fresh anyway.

I'll just brush my hair. One minute,' she promised, dragging her brush out of her shoulder-bag with one hand and holding up one finger with the other before she scampered into that amazing bathroom again.

'Isn't this place fabulous?' bubbled Tim's wife, Anne. 'It feels almost as if we've stepped onto the stage of a big-budget costume drama. We're the crowd of extras and all we need is the principal actors to make their entrance and the director to shout, "Action."'

At that precise moment Razak came striding in to join them and Lily shared a quiet laugh with Anne when she muttered, 'Oh, yes! Definitely leading-man material!'

'Please, everybody. Don't stand on ceremony,' he invited. 'The food has been set out as a buffet so you can help yourselves to whatever takes your fancy. And try a few things you don't recognise, too!'

'Hello, Lily. I'm so glad to see you again,' said a half-remembered voice behind her, and she turned to find Razak's brother waiting with a smile.

'Oh, Karim, it's lovely to see you, too!' she exclaimed. 'Can I introduce you to Anne? Her husband, Tim, is…*was* one of Razak's anaesthetists.'

She watched with a smile as Karim turned his charm on her companion but she could tell that there was something different about Razak's younger brother. He'd been such a laid-back character when she'd met him all those months ago. Today there was a suppressed air of excitement about him, almost as if he was ready to explode.

He turned back to her, for a moment apparently lost for words. 'I'm afraid I have some unfortunate information Lily,' he said biting his lip. 'It seems that your luggage has somehow been mislaid. I hope you will not mind that my sisters will put out some clothing for you to wear this evening?'

'Oh.' She blinked, wondering how her bag could have gone astray when it had been loaded by hand onto the private plane that had brought them here. 'But…my wash kit was in there, and my outfit for this evening.' Not that she'd been absolutely certain that she'd made the most flattering choice, but she hadn't wanted to ask the advice of any of her sisters because she would have had to tell them why it was so important to her to look cool, calm and collected.

'I promise, my sisters will see to everything. You have only to ask.' He gave her one of those smiles that was so like his elder brother's. 'I will see you later for the ceremony—after you have all been to the hospital.'

Surely he had meant that he would see her later at the hospital for the ceremony, Lily thought, her brain rearranging his words as she sampled a selection of the delicious food.

'This is almost like going on a school outing,' someone called out a short while later as they all embarked on a luxurious coach. 'Does anyone know how far away the hospital is?'

'The journey will take about twenty minutes,' the coach driver informed them. 'There will be many guests and much attention from television and newspapers but you are special guests of the family so you will have special place for ceremony.'

The finished centre looked even better than the architect's drawings had suggested, a pleasing mixture of traditional materials and modern methods that certainly didn't look out of place beside the rest of the hospital, with rapidly climbing plants already softening the outline.

Inside was even better, with no expense spared to make this a facility that would live up to everything its patients might need. Every detail seemed to be perfect, from something as mundane as the choice of floor coverings to the most high-tech, computer-controlled MRI and CT scanners. The fully equipped rehab department alone was enough to make them all green with envy.

But it was the theatres that that drew most admiration from the team and no little measure of envy, in spite of the fact that they'd been working in the most modern ones in their own hospital for the last few months.

'So, how many of you would like to sign up?' Razak teased, clearly delighted with the way his dream had taken shape. 'We already have staff in the old orthopaedic department in the main hospital and they will be moving in here with me, but until they have been trained in the parallel theatre system the way you have…' He shook his head sorrowfully. 'They will be nothing like you people for a long time to come.'

'They'll *never* be like us,' Tim contradicted, to cheers of agreement from his colleagues. 'We're completely unique and special.'

Lily had a lump in her throat when she realised that Tim had spoken nothing less than the truth. They were a special team, but that was largely because Razak had made them into a team with his own drive and enthusiasm.

Long before he'd come to the end of his contract they'd had the satisfaction of catching up completely with the outstanding list of patients waiting for operations. No one now had to wait longer than two or three weeks after their initial consultation for their operation, and they'd even had enough theatre time spare to operate on their colleagues' patients when even their lists become unconscionably long.

She had a sad feeling that their department would never be the same now he had left it, even though Geoff would be continuing with the same operating system.

The dedication ceremony was very similar to their own, all those months ago, but this time the VIP cutting the ribbon was someone she'd actually met and spoken to—Razak's father.

He still looked a little frail but he was looking so much better than the first time she'd seen him, in a hospital bed hooked up to wires and drips after surgery.

To her surprise, once the ceremony was over he beckoned her over to speak to him.

'I am so pleased to see you here in my country again,' he said, as he looped her hand through his elbow and patted it as he set off for a gentle walk around the lushly landscaped grounds. 'Are you pleased to be here again? Do you like my country?'

'I haven't seen very much of it,' she temporised honestly, but there was something in his expression that encouraged her to say more than the usual platitudes, to tell him about the deeper impressions it had made on her.

'When we flew in this morning the sun was just rising and spilling across the land and I was struck by how ancient and...untamed it looked, harsh and stark even. But then we flew over the river valley and it was so vividly green that it almost hurt your eyes.'

'Is it a country you could live in?' he persisted gently, and her heart ached with the knowledge that, much as she would love to work here, she could never bear to see Razak every day knowing… 'Perhaps you prefer your own, with its jumble of fields and hedges and patches of lush landscape broken up by neat little villages and towns.'

Lily was silent for so long that he stopped walking and tightened his hold on her hand, waiting until she was ready to answer with the words that came directly from her heart.

'It isn't the country you live in that matters,' she said softly, an ocean of sadness lapping around her heart. 'It's the person who shares that country with you.'

He nodded once. 'A wise head on young shoulders,' he said softly. 'Come! It is time to go back. There are more ceremonies before this day is over and I am an old man who doesn't like to go to bed too late.'

He insisted that she keep him company in the limousine that took them home and just before they parted company in the great entrance hall he tightened his grip on her hand for one last moment.

'You will have important decisions to make soon,' he said seriously. 'Just remember that sometimes it is important to listen to your heart as well as your head.'

She was still wondering what he was talking about when she arrived back in her room, pleased that she'd actually managed to find her own way, and found several packages waiting for her on the end of the bed.

'Phew!' She whistled when she saw the designer names printed on them. 'This is better than Christmas,' she gasped when she saw the sets of silky underwear and nightwear, then guilt struck her. This was all so much better quality than the ordinary chain-store stuff in her missing bag. The shoes, too, were glove-soft leather with the small neat heel she preferred and exactly her size. The fact that she'd been taller than most of her contemporaries and that she had to spend so many hours in a day on her feet had put her off wearing anything higher many years ago. Razak must have told someone that, although where they would have found something so perfect in such a short space of time…

The last package was a large flat unmarked box that revealed several layers of tissue paper protecting the most beautiful dress she'd ever seen.

Somewhere between a slim-fitting coat and an evening dress, it was floor-length and had a wealth of sumptuous embroidery around the neckline and down the front that exactly matched the ivory colour of the fabric.

A tap at the door revealed Faria's smiling face.

'I will help you to get ready,' she announced, as she carried in an armful of toiletries. 'First, the hair.'

For a moment Lily was astonished by the young woman's take-charge attitude. There certainly wasn't a trace of the self-effacing persona she'd shown earlier as she beckoned her towards the bathroom.

Lily hesitated, unaccustomed to allowing people to do things for her that she was perfectly capable of doing for herself, but then something inside her told her to just let go and enjoy the opportunity and she relinquished control for however long it took for Faria to achieve her aims.

It was more than an hour before her determined taskmistress was satisfied and finally stepped back to allow Lily her first look at her efforts.

'Oh, Faria,' she breathed, when she caught sight of the vision in the mirror, and even the fact that she was surrounded by the scent of jasmine from the perfume the young woman had applied couldn't dim her delight.

Whatever the young woman had used on her hair—henna, perhaps—had brought out highlights of bronze, copper and gold that she'd never seen before in her dull broomhandle-brown hair, and as for the make-up she'd applied so delicately…

'You can hardly see that it's there, even when you look closely,' she murmured, leaning towards the mirror. 'But whatever you've done makes my eyes look so big and the shape of my face…'

For the first time she could see a resemblance with her mother and her so much prettier sisters. Had it been there all the time, if only she'd been bothered to look, just waiting for the right touch?

'And now your dress,' Faria prompted urgently, after a quick glance at her watch. 'You must be ready in time.'

Lily was certain no one would notice if she didn't turn up in time for whatever ceremony was to take place, but her delicate despot obviously had other ideas as she helped her into the gorgeous creation and fastened the row of real pearl buttons that ran all the way from neck to hem.

The shoes were every bit as comfortable as they'd looked, but she barely had time for more than a stunned moment or two marvelling at the exquisite picture she saw in the mirror before there was a knock at the door.

'Oh! It is time!' Faria exclaimed, and hesitated for just a second before she leant forward to brush her cheek against Lily's. 'I wish you much happiness,' she said, just before the knock came a second time and she raced to open it.

Lily wasn't sure who she'd been expecting—someone to tell her that it was time for them all to gather for this latest ceremony, perhaps—but it certainly hadn't been Razak.

'What are *you* doing here?' she demanded on a squeak of disbelief, her heart breaking all over again when she saw how wonderful he looked and knew that after today he would be for ever out of her reach. 'Shouldn't you be getting ready?'

Faria had told her while she'd been completing the beauty rituals that his father would be making his formal announcement confirming his son's eventual succession just before the marriage ceremony.

Until that moment Lily had thought she had at least another few hours to marshal her self-control before she had to watch the man she loved marry someone else. Now she knew it was a matter of minutes away and to have him here, in her room, with those dark, dark eyes gleaming as they gazed at her, was almost more than she could stand without breaking down, and she refused to do that in front of him.

'Ah, my jasmine flower,' he said in the husky tone that she would remember for ever. 'So beautiful. So perfect.'

She swallowed hard. 'What are you doing here, Razak?' she demanded, her voice shakier than she would have liked.

'I have come for three reasons,' he said, and to her surprise she heard a hint of nervousness in his voice. What did he have to be nervous about? Curiosity alone kept her listening when logic should have had her sending him away.

'First, I must make an apology,' he said. 'It is a long overdue apology, but that does not mean it is any less deeply felt. My behaviour that night was more than regrettable, it was…inexcusable.'

Lily had to consciously lock her knees to stop herself collapsing. She'd thought her heart couldn't hurt any more but to hear that he regretted what had happened between them was…

'I am *not* apologising for making love to you,' he declared bluntly, stopping her thoughts in their tracks. 'I do not regret a single moment…a single caress… Just the way I behaved when I discovered that I was the first man you had ever permitted to be with you in that way.'

'So, why did you…?' she whispered, more confused than ever. If he didn't regret what had happened, why had he…? 'No!' She shook her head sharply. 'Don't say anything more. It doesn't really matter why you rejected me, does it? None of it does. When your mother told me about Dita I understood that it had only been some sort of game for you.'

'Ah!' he said, as though a puzzle had just been solved. 'And Mother doubtless also spoke to you about the duties and expectations of the first-born son.'

Something in her face gave him his answer and he flung his arms out impatiently.

'Oh, Lily, how could you ever believe for a minute that I would give up being a doctor? Surely you know that it is part of who I am?'

'I said that, too. But she said that you would never go against your father's wishes.'

'True. But that doesn't mean that I wouldn't try to change his mind, or that he is so stubborn that he wouldn't see that Karim is infinitely better suited to be his successor.'

'Karim?' She smiled at last, remembering the suppressed air of excitement that had surrounded his younger brother earlier. 'That's what your father's going to announce tonight?'

'Yes, but he's also hoping to make another announcement—that of the marriage of his first-born son to the woman he loves.'

'Dita,' she said dully, her heart suddenly a leaden lump in her chest again.

'No, *not* Dita, you stubborn woman!' he exclaimed,

striding towards her impatiently. 'If you had ever let me get close enough to explain I would have told you that Dita and I have never loved each other as anything other than friends. It is *Karim* she has always loved, as he loves her.'

Karim? 'But the betrothal?'

'That crazy betrothal—and my mother's insistence that it should be honoured—has caused many problems for all of us. Dita and her family have no problem with the fact that she will be marrying Karim instead, especially now he is to be my father's heir. And I have no problem releasing her from the arrangement because my heart has belonged to someone else ever since the first day she walked into my department and I saw those serious grey-blue eyes.'

'You…? W-what?' she stammered, as her knees once more threatened to let her down.

'Ah, Lily, sometimes I thought you must be the only person who did *not* know how I feel about you,' he said, as he finally took that last step that separated them and took her in his arms. 'After the disastrous ending to that night, you were so determined not to let me get near you that all I could do was honour your wishes. But that didn't mean that I didn't want to spend as much time with you as possible, so I devised a plan to court you by giving you what you *did* want from me…the benefit of my experience as an orthopaedic surgeon to help you with your own career.'

'Courtship among the blood and bones,' she said on a shaky chuckle. 'But that still doesn't explain why… If you say you…you cared for me—'

'*Loved* you,' he corrected firmly.

'Then why did you reject me like that when you discovered—?'

'I did *not* reject you,' he refuted heatedly, cupping both hands around her face and tilting it up to his.

Those dark eyes were so close that she could have counted every one of his equally dark eyelashes, but she was also close enough to know that there was no trace of evasion in them as he continued. 'I was so amazed and delighted and possessive in a totally primitive way and…there were all these thoughts in my head and all I could be certain of was that I wanted to be married to you before I truly made you mine.'

'Married?' she gasped, wide-eyed, that word leaping out at her even as the months of hurt disappeared without trace. 'You want to *marry* me?'

'Yes, I want to marry you,' he said, and brushed a tender kiss across her lips. 'I want to marry you in a dress the same rich colour of pearls as your skin, with traditional embroidery to decorate it and buttons all the way down the front that will make me want to scream with frustration as I try to undo them to get my first look at my bride in the privacy of our bedroom.

'I want to make our vows of forever in front of my family and yours, with all our colleagues there to wish us well and Chloe as your bridesmaid and—'

'Razak?' She put her fingers over his mouth to silence him for a moment as a giddy sense of unreality swept over her. He couldn't possibly mean what this sounded like—that he wanted them to marry *today*?

She didn't even have to put her question into words. Once more it was as if he'd read her mind.

'Say yes, my love,' he whispered with his heart in his eyes. 'I have taken the biggest gamble of my life and have invited them all here in the hope that you might love me enough to accept.'

'They're all here?' she gasped. 'You brought my family here, too? But I spoke to Iris yesterday and she never said a word. And Chloe?'

'You are not angry that they...*we* have kept secrets from you?'

She was having difficulty grasping the enormity of what had been going on without her knowledge, not least the lengths this wonderful man would go to in order to prove his love.

'No.' She shook her head, staring up at his handsome face in the realisation that everything she wanted was actually right in front of her. 'I'm amazed, but not angry.'

'And...you will marry me? Please? If I promise that I will never keep secrets from you again?'

'You only have to promise to love me,' she said with a shaky smile as her heart overflowed.

'Is that a yes?' he prompted. 'I promise I will love you for ever but you have to say the word.'

'Yes, Razak,' she said, feeling a wide smile of joy spread across her face. 'Yes, I love you and, yes, I will marry you.'

'Then let us not waste another moment,' he said fervently, ushering her towards the door. 'My father is waiting to hear whether there is to be a second wedding today, our guests are waiting to know that they have not travelled all this way for nothing and I have waited the longest of all, dreaming of this day when you will finally be mine.'

'As you will be mine,' she reminded him gently, her feet barely seeming to touch the floor as they hurried along the corridor towards their destiny.

'A true partnership,' he agreed several moments later, as

he paused briefly outside the enormous doors that separated them from the hubbub of voices waiting for them on the other side. 'In the operating theatre, in our marriage bed and in every other part of our lives, you are the only wife I will ever need.'

He bent his head to give her a kiss to seal their promises then swung the doors open for them to step into their future together.

'They look so happy,' Lily said from the secluded corner they'd found as she and Razak watched Karim and Dita circle the room to greet each of their guests. The marble column threw a shadow substantial enough to hide both of them from most eyes amid the aftermath of the feast and supported his shoulders as he cradled her against his chest.

'They will be good for each other and for our country,' Razak said seriously. 'Not that my mother will ever entirely agree.' Lily's eyes were drawn to where her parents were speaking to Razak's father and mother, relieved to see them both laugh aloud at something her father had said. After her solitary conversation with his mother, she'd been convinced that such a happy scene would never be possible. Her sisters, too, were obviously enjoying every moment of their stay in such luxurious surroundings and were openly delighted that she'd married a man she truly loved.

'You are happy, my jasmine flower?' he murmured for her ears alone, the words hidden under the happy sounds of the gathering in front of them. Lily looked up into those dark, dark eyes that now revealed openly how much she was loved by this special man. The glimpses she'd caught when he'd been watching her over his surgical mask were nothing when compared to the blaze that warmed her now.

'Completely happy,' she said as she rested her head against his shoulder. 'I just can't believe how you managed to organise everything without anyone letting me know what was going on.'

'They were very understanding of my need for secrecy—I told each of them that my ego would never recover if it were ever known that I went to so much trouble only to have the woman of my dreams turn me down,' he said with a gleam in his eye, then returned a more serious answer. 'Mostly it was Karim and Dita's doing. When they went to her father and mine to tell them they wanted to be married, it left me free to choose my own bride. And then it was just a matter of finding an excuse to get everybody from work over here. As for your family…' He smiled reminiscently. 'One day you must ask your father about the day I came to ask for your hand in marriage. He told me that he appreciated the gesture, but that your hand belonged to you, and if I wanted it I was going to have to ask the owner in person.'

Lily chuckled, more relieved than she would ever admit that this day had turned out so differently from the way she'd feared it would. She'd honestly believed that she would have to sit there with her heart breaking, watching Razak and Dita…

'Lily?' said a voice at her elbow, and she couldn't help stiffening when she turned to see Razak's mother standing there. 'This is not what I wanted for my son,' she said, her heavy accent making the words seem very blunt. 'All his life I expected…hoped—'

'Mother…' Razak interrupted with a warning tone, but she threw him a quelling glance before fixing those dark eyes on Lily again.

'In all his life, not even on the day he became a doctor,

have I ever seen my son look so happy as he does today,' she declared, and Lily was stunned to see the glitter of tears in her eyes. 'And I am glad that he has found the wife to suit him even better than the one we found for him. I just hope…' She paused uncertainly for a second before continuing in a rush. 'I just hope that the two of you won't be too busy working at the hospital to give me some grandchildren.'

Lily felt a blush work its way up her throat and into her cheeks and desperately wanted to hide her face. Luckily Razak was answering for them both.

'Actually, Mother, Lily and I urgently need to have a conversation about that,' he said with a wicked gleam in his dark eyes just for her. 'You will make our apologies to everyone and thank them all for making this such a memorable day, won't you?'

'But, Razak, you can't just leave…' the elegant woman remonstrated, clearly scandalised by such a breach of protocol.

'Mother, relax,' he said gently, and kissed her cheek. 'I don't think anyone will really mind and I've waited long enough. I need to be alone with Lily.' And he wrapped his arm around Lily's shoulders and urged her towards the small door hidden in the corner.

'Where are we going?' she asked, when his hurried pace almost had her running to keep up with him.

'To hide ourselves away from everyone and everything,' he said, as he led her along what were probably the back stairs and corridors that helped the staff to remain largely invisible as they went about their duties. And then he was opening to door to the suite in which she'd prepared for what had unexpectedly become the happiest day of her life.

This time the bedroom was softly lit by candles that scented the air around them with the smell of jasmine as he turned the key in the lock. Somewhere in the background her favourite jazz was playing as he took her in his arms.

'Is it time for us to talk about those grandchildren your mother wants?' she asked, as every nerve in her body quivered in a mixture of uncertainty and anticipation. She had imagined this day so often, believing that it was only a hopeless dream.

'I have a much better idea,' he said, his voice rich with desire as his long agile fingers toyed with the first of the many buttons fastening the front of her dress before slipping the pearl smoothly through the embroidered hole. 'If you agree, I think we should just let our hearts and desires take us where they will.'

Lily knew exactly where her heart and her desires wanted to take her, though her fingers were trembling when they reached for the first of Razak's buttons.

'I think that the time for talking is over,' she whispered, surprised to hear how husky and inviting her voice sounded. 'You have always been so good at demonstrating new techniques to me in the operating theatre. I think now is a perfect time for a practical demonstration…or two.'

She gasped when he growled in response and swept her off her feet to stride over to the sumptuous bed she'd imagined sharing with him, then smiled with delight when he proceeded to make all her dreams come true.

1206 Gen Std HB

JANUARY 2007 HARDBACK TITLES

ROMANCE™

Title	Author	ISBN
Royally Bedded, Regally Wedded	*Julia James*	0 263 19556 2
The Sheikh's English Bride	*Sharon Kendrick*	0 263 19557 0
Sicilian Husband, Blackmailed Bride	*Kate Walker*	0 263 19558 9
At the Greek Boss's Bidding	*Jane Porter*	0 263 19559 7
The Spaniard's Marriage Demand	*Maggie Cox*	0 263 19560 0
The Prince's Convenient Bride	*Robyn Donald*	0 263 19561 9
One-Night Baby	*Susan Stephens*	0 263 19562 7
The Rich Man's Reluctant Mistress	*Margaret Mayo*	0 263 19563 5
Cattle Rancher, Convenient Wife	*Margaret Way*	0 263 19564 3
Barefoot Bride	*Jessica Hart*	0 263 19565 1
Their Very Special Gift	*Jackie Braun*	0 263 19566 X
Her Parenthood Assignment	*Fiona Harper*	0 263 19567 8
The Maid and the Millionaire	*Myrna Mackenzie*	0 263 19568 6
The Prince and the Nanny	*Cara Colter*	0 263 19569 4
A Doctor Worth Waiting For	*Margaret McDonagh*	0 263 19570 8
Her L.A. Knight	*Lynne Marshall*	0 263 19571 6

HISTORICAL ROMANCE™

Title	Author	ISBN
Innocence and Impropriety	*Diane Gaston*	0 263 19748 4
Rogue's Widow, Gentleman's Wife	*Helen Dickson*	0 263 19749 2
High Seas to High Society	*Sophia James*	0 263 19750 6

MEDICAL ROMANCE™

Title	Author	ISBN
A Father Beyond Compare	*Alison Roberts*	0 263 19784 0
An Unexpected Proposal	*Amy Andrews*	0 263 19785 9
Sheikh Surgeon, Surprise Bride	*Josie Metcalfe*	0 263 19786 7
The Surgeon's Chosen Wife	*Fiona Lowe*	0 263 19787 5

1206 Gen Std LP

JANUARY 2007 LARGE PRINT TITLES

ROMANCE™

Mistress Bought and Paid For	*Lynne Graham*	0 263 19415 9
The Scorsolini Marriage Bargain	*Lucy Monroe*	0 263 19416 7
Stay Through the Night	*Anne Mather*	0 263 19417 5
Bride of Desire	*Sara Craven*	0 263 19418 3
Married Under the Italian Sun	*Lucy Gordon*	0 263 19419 1
The Rebel Prince	*Raye Morgan*	0 263 19420 5
Accepting the Boss's Proposal	*Natasha Oakley*	0 263 19421 3
The Sheikh's Guarded Heart	*Liz Fielding*	0 263 19422 1

HISTORICAL ROMANCE™

The Bride's Seduction	*Louise Allen*	0 263 19379 9
A Scandalous Situation	*Patricia Frances Rowell*	0 263 19380 2
The Warlord's Mistress	*Juliet Landon*	0 263 19381 0

MEDICAL ROMANCE™

The Midwife's Special Delivery	*Carol Marinelli*	0 263 19331 4
A Baby of His Own	*Jennifer Taylor*	0 263 19332 2
A Nurse Worth Waiting For	*Gill Sanderson*	0 263 19333 0
The London Doctor	*Joanna Neil*	0 263 19334 9
Emergency in Alaska	*Dianne Drake*	0 263 19531 7
Pregnant on Arrival	*Fiona Lowe*	0 263 19532 5

0107 Gen Std HB

FEBRUARY 2007 HARDBACK TITLES

ROMANCE™

The Marriage Possession *Helen Bianchin* 978 0 263 19572 9
The Sheikh's Unwilling Wife *Sharon Kendrick* 978 0 263 19573 6
The Italian's Inexperienced Mistress *Lynne Graham* 978 0 263 19574 3
The Sicilian's Virgin Bride *Sarah Morgan* 978 0 263 19575 0
The Rich Man's Bride *Catherine George* 978 0 263 19576 7
Wife by Contract, Mistress by Demand *Carole Mortimer* 978 0 263 19577 4
Wife by Approval *Lee Wilkinson* 978 0 263 19578 1
The Sheikh's Ransomed Bride *Annie West* 978 0 263 19579 8
Raising the Rancher's Family *Patricia Thayer* 978 0 263 19580 4
Matrimony with His Majesty *Rebecca Winters* 978 0 263 19581 1
In the Heart of the Outback... *Barbara Hannay* 978 0 263 19582 8
Rescued: Mother-To-Be *Trish Wylie* 978 0 263 19583 5
The Sheikh's Reluctant Bride *Teresa Southwick* 978 0 263 19584 2
Marriage for Baby *Melissa McClone* 978 0 263 19585 9
City Doctor, Country Bride *Abigail Gordon* 978 0 263 19586 6
The Emergency Doctor's Daughter *Lucy Clark* 978 0 263 19587 3

HISTORICAL ROMANCE™

A Most Unconventional Courtship *Louise Allen* 978 0 263 19751 8
A Worthy Gentleman *Anne Herries* 978 0 263 19752 5
Sold and Seduced *Michelle Styles* 978 0 263 19753 2

MEDICAL ROMANCE™

His Very Own Wife and Child *Caroline Anderson* 978 0 263 19788 4
The Consultant's New-Found Family *Kate Hardy* 978 0 263 19789 1
A Child to Care For *Dianne Drake* 978 0 263 19790 7
His Pregnant Nurse *Laura Iding* 978 0 263 19791 4

0107 Gen Std LP

FEBRUARY 2007 LARGE PRINT TITLES

ROMANCE™

Title / Author	ISBN
Purchased by the Billionaire *Helen Bianchin*	978 0 263 19423 4
Master of Pleasure *Penny Jordan*	978 0 263 19424 1
The Sultan's Virgin Bride *Sarah Morgan*	978 0 263 19425 8
Wanted: Mistress and Mother *Carol Marinelli*	978 0 263 19426 5
Promise of a Family *Jessica Steele*	978 0 263 19427 2
Wanted: Outback Wife *Ally Blake*	978 0 263 19428 9
Business Arrangement Bride *Jessica Hart*	978 0 263 19429 6
Long-Lost Father *Melissa James*	978 0 263 19430 2

HISTORICAL ROMANCE™

Title / Author	ISBN
Mistaken Mistress *Margaret McPhee*	978 0 263 19382 4
The Inconvenient Duchess *Christine Merrill*	978 0 263 19383 1
Falcon's Desire *Denise Lynn*	978 0 263 19384 8

MEDICAL ROMANCE™

Title / Author	ISBN
The Sicilian Doctor's Proposal *Sarah Morgan*	978 0 263 19335 0
The Firefighter's Fiancé *Kate Hardy*	978 0 263 19336 7
Emergency Baby *Alison Roberts*	978 0 263 19337 4
In His Special Care *Lucy Clark*	978 0 263 19338 1
Bride at Bay Hospital *Meredith Webber*	978 0 263 19533 0
The Flight Doctor's Engagement *Laura Iding*	978 0 263 19534 7